"It's about Chad."

Zoey's breath caught in her throat. "Did you find him?"

"No," Eli answered. "There's a hit out on Chad."

She took her phone out and dialed Chad's number. The call went straight to voice mail.

Something was wrong...very wrong.

"It's going to be okay, Zoey."

She couldn't lose her brother. There was only one thing she could do—she had to kill whoever took the hit out on him.

"Who took the job?" she asked.

"It's an open contract." He paused. "Five million. But that's not all."

"What? What do you mean? Did someone already get to him?" Zoey stopped moving, but her blood pounded in her veins.

"Watch Dog took the contract."

"The company you work for?"

He nodded.

"Which operative is working the hit?"

He looked up at her, pain in his eyes. "I am."

HER ASSASSIN FOR HIRE

DANICA WINTERS

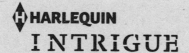

To Mac, don't worry, I'll keep bringing the cheese.

This series wouldn't have been possible without a great team of
people, including Melanie Calahan and Clare Wood, my #1k1hr
friends, Jill Marsal and the editors at Harlequin—thank you for all
your hard work.

Also, thank you to my readers. You keep me writing.

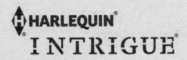

HARLEQUIN®
INTRIGUE®

Recycling programs
for this product may
not exist in your area.

ISBN-13: 978-1-335-13631-2

Her Assassin For Hire

Copyright © 2020 by Danica Winters

For questions and comments about the quality of this book,
please contact us at CustomerService@Harlequin.com.

Harlequin Enterprises ULC
22 Adelaide St. West, 40th Floor
Toronto, Ontario M5H 4E3, Canada
www.Harlequin.com

Printed in U.S.A.

Danica Winters is a multiple-award-winning, bestselling author who writes books that grip readers with their ability to drive emotion through suspense and occasionally a touch of magic. When she's not working, she can be found in the wilds of Montana, testing her patience while she tries to hone her skills at various crafts—quilting, pottery and painting are not her areas of expertise. She believes the cup is neither half-full nor half-empty, but it better be filled with wine. Visit her website at danicawinters.net.

Books by Danica Winters

Harlequin Intrigue

Stealth

Hidden Truth
In His Sights
Her Assassin For Hire

Mystery Christmas

Ms. Calculation
Mr. Serious
Mr. Taken

Smoke and Ashes
Dust Up with the Detective
Wild Montana

Visit the Author Profile page at Harlequin.com.

CAST OF CHARACTERS

Zoey Martin—Wild woman, tech genius, beautiful, smart, sexy and forever dangerous. Though she is constantly challenged by her family, she will do anything to keep those she loves safe.

Eli Wayne—A dark and brooding lone wolf who hates bureaucracy and injustice. Has seen too many victims get shafted when abusers walk away, killers plead out and thieves get a slap on the wrist while the victims of the crimes have their lives ripped apart. If he gets his way, he will make things right.

STEALTH—The Martins' private government contracting company, known for taking down those deemed unsavory by the US government and its many citizens.

Mindy Kohl—A socialite with a backbone and nerves of steel, Mindy is a woman not to be crossed. She and Zoey Martin have created a new philanthropic-based line of tactical gear meant to keep the innocent safe.

Jarrod Martin—Zoey's brother and Mindy's fiancé. Jarrod is a man who makes the rules and follows them to the letter. He's very organized and regimented, and completely ambivalent to the opinions of anyone besides those he cares about.

Chad Martin—Zoey's brother and the family clown. He takes very little seriously, but he is the man in the shadows who often controls far more than anyone expects—until he goes missing and is possibly killed.

Shaye Griest—Daughter of the Algerian prime minister, but she fell in love and married the wrong man—a decision that may or may not come back to haunt everyone around her.

Trish Martin—Zoey's sister who was killed in action in Turkey while STEALTH was running an undercover operation in which they infiltrated terrorist organizations through the illicit gun trade.

Fenrisulfr Bayural—The leader of the Bozkurtlar, or the Gray Wolves, a terrorist organization that works around the globe and leaves only murder and mayhem in their wake.

Chapter One

In life, there comes a point when all people are forced to pick a side and show who they really are. In the stories, it was always good versus evil—and those with the purest hearts won. However, in reality, nothing was ever that simple.

As a child, Zoey Martin had a favorite maple tree. It stood proud and unyielding in her family's front yard, a symbol of strength and longevity. She would spend hours climbing around, whispering her secrets into its bark and imagining her future…a future that would bring only happiness and success. Each dream was a bit different, but there was always the same ending—her, standing in front of a crowd of cheering fans, wearing the shining armor of a knight who had once again saved the innocent.

She had relied on the strength of the maple tree and over the years had almost come to take it for granted. It was always there, always shielding her as she hoped to shield others someday. In a way it was her hero.

One day, when she was nearly ten years old, the seemingly healthy limb she had been sitting on snapped beneath her. She had tumbled to the ground. Even now, so many years later, if she closed her eyes and concentrated, she could still hear her leg snapping as she struck the unyielding roots of the behemoth she had loved.

Over the years, when her first boyfriend cheated on her with her best friend, and later when her college boyfriend ghosted her, she thought back to her tree. It was her first hard-learned lesson in the wicked truths of trust—just because everything looked good from the outside, healthy even, it didn't mean its heart wasn't rotten.

Since then, Zoey Martin had been happy giving her trust to a few within her family. Her only heroes were their STEALTH team and their teams of courageous contractors.

Even limiting who she loved and trusted, ever since her sister's death, she felt herself tumbling to the ground. Her family's work in STEALTH, something she believed in so strongly, had pulled the stable branch out from under her family.

She'd had to move forward in the faith that she was sure she was bringing something positive to the world.

She tugged down the edge of her hot pink dress as she sauntered to the front of the tent. Her high heels clicked on the hardwood floor she had her staff put down just so her shoes wouldn't stick in the grass.

Today everything had to be perfect…especially her appearance.

Rubbing her lips together, ensuring her specially blended-to-match lipstick was in place, she turned to face her audience.

They looked bored, most checking their phones or staring longingly at the bar in the corner of the room. No doubt, the crowd was made up of gold-laden investors, soggy board members and straight-backed rivals. They all held their pints of beer or flutes of champagne like lifelines.

She couldn't wait to see their faces when the fun started.

So far, it had been two days of looking over the next year's models of top-of-the-line weaponry and tactical gear, speeches on the merits of self-protection and gun advocacy, and the late-night bar meetings that led to the next morning's multimillion-dollar deals. And she had one hell of a hangover.

Though their new line of tac-gear wasn't through the final phases of testing, they were taking orders. And after today, they were going to come flooding in.

There was a smattering of polite but unenthusiastic applause as she took out her prepared speech. She couldn't blame those in attendance for their lackluster response. Zoey wasn't one of her brothers. Until recently, it had always been Jarrod who had been the face of their private government contracting company, STEALTH, and no matter where Jarrod went, with his wide jaw and Dwayne "The Rock" Johnson brooding but sexy scowl, women and money followed. Thankfully her new friend and her brother's fiancée, Mindy Kohl, had put a stop to that party and Jarrod had settled down.

As Zoey cleared her throat, she checked to make sure her team was in place. The two men stood at each of the front corners of the tent in ready position, looking more like her private security team in their black suits and earpieces than what she had actually brought them here for.

She looked toward the waitstaff who were lowering the lights and closing the flaps to shut out the bright, midevening sun. The lights on the catwalk came to life, readying for the show.

A smile played at the corner of her lips as she adjusted her formfitting little hot pink dress one more time.

She didn't want to die…but if this was how she went out, at least she'd go out with one hell of a bang.

Either way, she was about to become infamous.

"Good afternoon, ladies and gentlemen," she started, looking out over the crowd as they found their seats. Most took out their phones like they were going to take notes, but in reality, were probably checking their backlog of emails from their days away from the office. "I appreciate you coming to the Heinrich and Kohl Alliance demonstration today."

It felt strange to have their new venture into tactical gear manufacturing umbrellaed under Mindy's company. But it was best to stay shielded from the public…especially when it came to her family and the worldwide manhunt that centered on them. Anonymity was their only saving grace.

"As some of you may know, our team has been working diligently over the last few months to bring you a new and innovative line of tactical gear and body armor." A man slipped into the tent and into one of the many open seats at the back of the room, carefully keeping to the shadows.

"Our decision," she said, thinking of Mindy, "to expand our manufacturing businesses to include self-protection and advocacy, came from a very honest place." And she honestly couldn't help but feel like she was using her sister Trish's death to profit—and she hated herself for it.

She cleared her throat as a few people turned off their phones and glanced up at her. "Last fall, my sister was shot and killed in the streets of Turkey." The last few voices in the crowd were silenced. "She had been there on a mission of her choosing. She was wearing body armor and was well equipped for the fight she knew she would face. But when the mission played out, her tac-gear and armor weren't enough to save her."

A woman near the catwalk shifted in her seat like talk of such a death at an arms show and convention was strictly taboo. Regardless of social mores, it was the truth. These people had to know death, and fear it, as they were the only constants in their line of work.

"Her death was a major blow not only to our family but to our business, as well. She was our linchpin, the one who always brought us together even in the hardest of times. She was our rock. And now she is gone." A lump rose in her throat, but she forced the emotional traitor to submit as she swallowed it away. "As you can imagine, thoughts of vengeance led to plans of retaliation against the group responsible. However, these thoughts were soon checked. Logic must reign when emotions threaten to rebel."

There were a few ill-timed chuckles, but she appreciated them.

"After careful planning, we chose to use her legacy to advocate for positive change, and this new line of tactical gear was designed in her honor. Through our work, we hope that no one else will ever have to endure such a tragedy."

She paused. There were no longer any dim lights from people playing on their cell phones in the crowd. Finally, she had everyone's rapt attention. *Perfect.*

"At H&K, we are in the final stages of testing our new lightweight phase armor we have affectionately dubbed Monster Wear. Today we will be taking preorders for our designs. Please feel free to see any one of our representatives, those with the white name tags, throughout the rest of the conference." She waved at two women who were staged beside the main entrance. "Without further ado, we are excited to unveil our full line of Monster Tactical Gear and Specialty Fashion for you today."

She gave a small clap, and the curtains opened from the side of the tent and their first model came out and strutted down the runway. He had on their line of UV protection sunglasses, their shellback tactical Cyclops plate carrier, tac pants and full duty gear. With his well-toned arms and buttery tan, the man looked like he'd just walked off the battlefield. *Perfect.*

Several more men and women followed, each wearing gear from the new line, but none wearing the best-of-the-best—at least not yet.

Zoey scanned the crowd. They seemed interested, but underwhelmed by the nearly generic gear on display. Which was, for now, just fine by her.

The man who had come in late stood up and moved closer to the catwalk. Zoey couldn't see his face, but something about his dark brown hair and V-shaped body seemed all too familiar. Maybe it was the way he roll-walked through the crowd, or how he seemed to be most comfortable in the shadows, but she was intrigued.

Her thoughts moved to Eli Wayne, her exboyfriend and STEALTH's former ghostlike point man. From the back, the man looked just like him.

The lump in her throat returned.

It was more than possible he would be here, sniffing around her demonstration in hopes of making contact with her. He'd always been like that, lurking in the darkness and waiting to sweep her off her feet just when she was at her most vulnerable—it was also one of the things that had made her fall for him in the first place.

In many ways, she missed him. And she hated him for breaking her heart. And... *Ugh... No.* She couldn't let thoughts of Eli mess with her head. She was here to do her job. To make her family proud, and to put him and their cursed past even further behind her.

She had to focus.

Ten different models moved through their line of gear, each doing quick changes in the back, before reappearing on the catwalk. A few in the crowd oohed and ahhed as the models rolled out.

As the time grew nearer to unveil their greatest achievements, the nervousness swelled within her. She took a series of deep breaths as she tried to control herself. This was just a simple event—a sales pitch. It was nothing in comparison to sitting behind the screen and running IT for her family as they infiltrated and took down an enemy encampment. Now, that was something to be nervous about. One poorly timed click of the button, one little sneeze, and she could blow away an entire village—or hurt one of her own.

And yet there she was, getting butterflies at a fashion show. Maybe she was more of a girlie girl than she had realized. Or maybe it was the thought of Eli being in the room that was really getting to her.

She ran her hands down her dress, trying to dry her palms.

Feeling this way was simply ridiculous. He wasn't here. He didn't care about her anymore. Even if he was here, he wouldn't waste his time by checking in on her.

"And finally," she said, as the last model slipped behind the curtain, "I'm proud to announce the arrival of our new and groundbreaking line of fashion... Please give a round of applause for our models wearing our new Level III ballistic protection Monster Wear."

The curtain opened and a man came out in a well-fitted black suit nearly identical to the Armani her men at the side doors wore.

She walked over to the model and gave him a smile. "If you note—" she lifted the fabric of the jacket and twisted it in her fingers "—the cloth moves and breathes just like regular cotton. It is thin, light and available in a variety of colors. No more need for steel plates and heavy, movement-restricting armor."

A few in the audience caught their breath.

Zoey waved the model on. He took off his jacket, revealing his white dress shirt. He glanced back at her and gave her a sly smile as he dropped his jacket to the ground. He leaped forward, his hands raised in the air, and he did a tight spiral backflip onto the ground, landing just in front of the woman seated in the front row.

There was a roar of applause.

Yes.

Money would be flowing in no time.

If they could sell just ten thousand button-up shirts, they would recoup their entire investment, and anything beyond would be gravy

She sent a silent prayer up to Trish, one begging for her forgiveness.

As the model weaved through the crowd, letting the audience touch and feel the Lycra-like cloth, the next model entered from the side. She wore a black pair of yoga pants and a white T-shirt. Nothing fancy, and nothing to indicate she was prepped for a fire-fight.

"We are proud at H&K to design clothing that meets everyday needs for all. We don't simply create clothing for high-profile events and celebrities, but we also want to protect those who are just like us—those out there risking their lives for the greater good."

Several models followed the woman as the crowd jostled in their seats for a better view. People were slipping in from the back entrance and, as there were no longer any seats available, standing room became a premium.

As the last model disappeared, the crowd moved to their feet with applause.

"Thank you," Zoey said, glancing over to her

guards, who now looked more nervous than ever. "We appreciate your support in our continuing effort to bring safety to those who most need it."

A woman's scream pierced through the air.

Zoey turned to her right. There, just a few yards away, one of her guards raised his gun. He didn't hesitate as he pointed it straight at her center mass and pulled the trigger.

The bullet struck true.

She crumpled to the ground as pain flooded her senses. "It's okay, everyone. He works for me." She struggled to catch her breath.

Her hands moved to her chest. A trickle of blood seeped between her fingers.

We should have done more testing.

Or maybe Trish is calling me out for using her death to profit. If she was still here, I would tell her this was for her...all for her...

The world spun as Zoey tumbled downward and darkness swallowed her whole.

Chapter Two

What in the hell was that woman thinking, having her man shoot her to demonstrate one of her products?

Eli raced to the front of the tent and elbowed his way through the throngs of people who had rushed to help Zoey Martin.

Damn that woman.

He couldn't believe she would ever do something so foolish, so brash. Then again, should he really be surprised? All she ever cared about was being at the center of everything—attention, plans, a firefight—it didn't matter. It was Zoey Martin's way or no way at all.

Damn her.

And damn himself for thinking he could come here and walk away from her unscathed. Whenever he was near Zoey, he should know something bad was bound to happen.

If she was dead…he'd kill the man who'd pulled the trigger.

Who would have ever gone through with such a stupid publicity stunt?

Zoey lay in a fetal position as he got to her, her pink dress pulled up high on her thigh and exposing a little pair of black shorts. Her side rose and fell as she breathed, and aside from her lying there, and him having watched her being shot, she didn't look too much the worse for wear.

He pushed the crowd back from her, yelling at them to give her some space. He knelt down in front of her. "Zoey?"

Her eyes were closed and her lips were pursed as though she were trying to Lamaze her way through the pain. Even doing that, he'd be damned if she still wasn't one of the most beautiful women he'd ever seen. And *that* dress…

He held his chuckle as he realized once again he had found himself in trouble because of the perfect dress…and once again it was on Zoey, the woman his world had revolved around just two years ago.

Oh, how the mighty fall.

Zoey's eyes fluttered open, revealing her caramel-colored eyes. If only she were half as sweet as those eyes looked.

"Eli?" she said, her voice ragged with pain. As she moved to sit up he could see the blood on her fingers.

His heart dropped. She was really actually hurt.

His anger morphed into panic. "Zoey, we need to get you out of here and to the hospital. Do you think I can move you?" He leaned in and moved her hand.

There was a crushed slug embedded into the fabric of her dress.

Though he had heard rumors about the bulletproof capabilities of her new clothing line, he hadn't truly believed it until now. It seemed unfathomable that something like this was possible.

"Holy crap, Zoe..." he said. His breath escaped him as he reached down and pulled the slug from her dress.

The pink fabric was still in place, with not even a single tear. Where the bullet had impacted, there was a bit of blood seeping up and through the fabric. How could something stop a bullet, but then let blood through?

He stared as he tried to make sense of it until he finally pulled himself back to the task at hand.

"Zoey, are you okay? Can you move?" he asked.

She stared at him. "Eli, what in the hell are you doing here?" She moved to sit up. "You... You shouldn't have come."

"And you shouldn't have done what you just did." He gave her a hand and she pulled herself to standing. As their fingers touched, he couldn't help but be a little surprised that she had taken him up on his offer of help. She must have been hurting.

She pulled her hand from his. With a nod of acknowledgment, she made her way back up to the podium.

"Everyone," she said, clearing her throat and forcing herself to stand straight. "Everyone, please quiet down," she said over the manic cacophony of sound. "Excuse me."

The room silenced.

"As you can see, our new Monster Wear has the capability to stop a bullet at close range, all while being cool, comfortable and stylish," she said, stepping out just slightly so all could see her dress. "I am fine."

"You're bleeding!" someone in the crowd yelled.

"I said our clothing was bulletproof, I didn't say being shot would be pain-free." Zoey laughed, the sound tight and high like it hurt for her to breathe. "Like I always say, if you can't handle a bee sting then you need to stay out of the nest."

Eli shook his head.

Once again, he felt as if she had played him for a fool. Why did he have to be so stupid when it came to Zoey Martin?

He turned, about to walk out.

"Can we all give my assistant who was willing to pull the trigger, at my request, a big round of applause? And can we also please do the same for Mr. Eli Wayne for coming to the rescue of a lady?" She motioned in his direction and gave him her perfect, sexy smile… the one that always drew him back into her nest.

Applause filled the tent. Heat rose in his cheeks as men came up and patted him on the shoulder. He wasn't a hero. And though Zoey put on one hell of an act, she definitely wasn't a lady…at least not in the bedroom.

Almost as if she could read his mind, Zoey reached up and unzipped her dress. The fabric gripped her body and she had to roll it down in order to get it off her. Beneath the dress were those little black shorts and a black sports bra and nothing else.

His mind went to the last night they had spent together. What had it been, two years ago now? Sometimes their breakup seemed like a lifetime ago and then on days like this, it seemed like only yesterday.

He could still recall the way she smelled after her runs, a mixture of fresh air, sweat and strength. And when she was happy, her voice always took on a special lilt as though whatever she was saying was just for him. That was one thing he missed the most, the way she had always made him feel like he was the only man she had ever loved. And yet, he was left with nothing but a broken heart and fantasies of what could have been.

Oh, Zoey… Why did she do this to him?

She turned and smiled at him as her hand moved down her waist and rested gently on her hip.

His body disobeyed his mind and he could feel himself stirring to life in all the wrong places at the sight of her half-naked body.

The last time he had seen her this unclothed, it hadn't taken but a matter of seconds to get her into nothing at all. He could still remember the way she had tasted of salt and sweat on his lips as they made love. They had been on a takedown outside Tikrit, working a small village where a group of high-grade mercenaries, or mercs, had been holed up.

As he closed his eyes, he could almost feel the sand that had stuck to her skin as he worked his fingers down to her navel.

He stiffened further.

No.

He couldn't think of anything sultry about Zoey. No. She had watched his heart break and left him standing alone, without a job, without a home, without a family and completely adrift.

No matter what, he couldn't forgive her for all she had done to him and the wreckage she had left in his life.

"If you look," she said, motioning to her midsection, "the bullet left a bruise and an abrasion, but nothing more." She wiped her hands together in a feeble attempt to hide the blood that stained them.

She was swarmed by questions and she took her time answering each one.

He was relieved as a guard brought her a robe and she pulled it on over her body.

She was fine. She would always be just fine. She was the epitome of resilience.

He turned to leave, but Zoey waved to him as she ended the questions and bid goodbye to the crowd. He turned away, not wanting to once again do her bidding, but his resolve weakened. At the very least, before he left, he could make sure that she really was okay.

She could get up there and say she wasn't hurt all she wanted, but that didn't mean there wasn't some kind of internal damage from taking a hit like that. She was all show.

And he had always been the one to make sure that she wasn't faking things so much that she couldn't find her way back to reality.

Which made him wonder if that was part of the reason she had chosen this conference to unveil her new gear. She had to have known he would be here, hoping to catch sight of her. She had probably even known he would come to her rescue.

Maybe she missed him just as much as he missed her.

Wait. No. He didn't miss her or her stupid pink hair, or her wide-set dark-lined eyes, or her watermelon-colored lips that usually tasted of her mint sugar-free gum. And he definitely didn't miss the way she had loved to fall asleep in the crook of his arm, making his arm go to sleep and then later throb with pain when she finally rolled to her side in their bed.

Yep. He didn't miss her at all.

Damn it.

As the crowd started to dissipate, she made her way over to where he stood at the back of the tent.

She tugged her robe tighter around her body, like she was suddenly self-conscious in his presence.

"You're welcome," he said, fully aware from the slightly pursed look on her face that the last thing she wanted to say to him was thank you.

"I didn't tell you to come here." She brushed her pink hair out of her face. Up close, he couldn't help but notice it was dyed the same shade of Barbie pink as her dress.

"Uh-huh," he grumbled. "You and I both know Billings is my territory."

"I thought you were out working for a new crew. I don't keep tabs on you, Eli." She crossed her arms over her chest, but as she moved her arm over the place she'd taken the hit, she winced with pain and lowered her arms.

"Why did you do such a stupid thing? What would have happened if your guy had missed? What if he'd shot you in the neck?" He reached over and put his finger against the place that the bullet had struck. "You could have died, Zoey."

She moved away from his touch. "This was hardly the first time, or the last, that I stood at the edge of death, Eli. This is our life—dealing with pain. And you know it just as well as I do."

And perhaps that was one of the main reasons he was glad they really were no longer together.

"It doesn't mean it's okay to make stupid choices."

"Doing my job isn't making a stupid choice." She leaned against the back of a chair. "I believe in the H&K products and its people." Her tone made it clear he didn't make her short list.

"Why did you want me to stay, Zoey?" He wasn't about to stand there and continue to be her whipping boy. "Is it just so you can tell me all the reasons we don't work anymore?"

Some of her antagonism seemed to seep out as she dropped her shoulders and sighed. "I…" she began. "Actually, I was hoping you would give me the slug. You know. For marketing and such." She stuck out her hand like a child asking for a quarter.

"Yeah, right." He reached into his pocket where he had dropped the spent bullet. With it came his business card.

He stared at the card in his fingers, but before he could think about tucking it back into his pocket, Zoey reached out and took them both.

"I… Uh…" She paused, collecting herself. She pulled out her phone. "I guess I should thank you properly for what you did back there."

She opened up her phone and punched in his number, then moved to her calendar like she was thinking about finding a time that would work for them to go out. On her schedule he could make out the words *Therapy appointment* set for tomorrow, and beneath was an address.

He looked up at her as she tapped through her schedule.

Was she really interested in going out with him? And was she really going to a therapist?

Did it have something to do with what had happened to them?

He was glad she was seeing someone, but Zoey

had never been the kind to open up. Maybe she had changed since she had left him.

"Hey," he said. "By the way, I'm sorry to hear about your sister. She was always wonderful to me. If I had it to do all over again, I would happily work by her side."

Zoey stopped with her phone and looked up at him, staring at him like she was looking for some kind of meaning to what he'd just said. "Are you saying you want to come back to STEALTH?" Her voice was choked.

"No. It's just… I meant…" Now, he was the one stammering. It wasn't that he hadn't missed his old job and the STEALTH family, but she didn't want him there and they both knew it.

Why was any interaction between them so awkward?

"I meant that I just wish nothing had happened to Trish. We lost a good one with her."

She nodded, but her gaze stayed locked on his face.

A blonde woman wove through the chairs over toward them, and Zoey finally looked away.

"I have to go, Eli." She handed him back his card. "But maybe…someday, we could catch up."

Catching up? Was she for real? They both knew after this moment it was unlikely they would ever see one another again.

And the thought, just like the woman who was walking away from him, threatened to rip out his heart.

Chapter Three

The ride back to the Widow Maker Ranch seemed even longer than she had remembered. She had driven through entire countries faster than she had driven across the state of Montana. The conference had gone well, and she was getting texts and alerts about new orders that were coming through the doors, but her mind kept circling back to Eli. Maybe it was his fault that the drive had seemed to take so long.

He had a way of making everything in her life more complicated. It was a good thing that she was putting hundreds of miles between them.

But it had been stupid of her to take his phone number. She had excised him ever so precisely from her life already, and now she had allowed him to slip back in. What was wrong with her?

She'd always stuck to the Band-Aid breakup model—one quick rip and throw it away. She was too old to make such a stupid mistake and let him reappear. His coming back would only open up all those old wounds. Not that everything had been bad between them. Some days had been incredible, while others—especially at the end—had been pure hell.

One time, when they had been in the belly of Italy, they had taken a contract on a set of twins. The brothers they had been hired to kill had been members of a notorious terrorist organization, in so deep that they had helped establish the group's core documents and constitution. Thanks to their work, the group had grown to over five thousand international members and was responsible for the deaths of over two hundred civilians—men, women and one child.

During the strike, she and Eli had been forced to camp out under the stars while they waited for the brothers to return to their compound. While she had tracked the brothers' phones, she and Eli had started out talking about throwaway things— the weather, locations and food preferences. After a few hours, however, something changed and they began talking about those things in life that make a person unique—family, beliefs, culture. He had even told her about growing up in rural Idaho, near Boise, where he had learned to shoot a BB gun and take care of his family's bevy of animals.

The number one rule of their occupation as hit men was that everything was a secret. To open up, even the tiniest bit meant death.

But as they had talked, she forgot that rule. She was surprised to learn that he was such a sucker for animals. Maybe it was the thought of him holding a puppy, but whatever reservations she had about their growing intimacy quickly disappeared.

Everything between them changed. They became a team. And then that team mentality had taken another turn, and taking aim at killers and thieves had turned into taking aim at each other's hearts.

She had been a fool to get involved with him. When she kissed him she had stripped her life of one of her best friends and one of just a select few that she had trusted.

The only other person she had trusted in the same way had been her sister. When Trish had been alive, Zoey had been able to turn to her, to talk to her a bit about the things that were going on in her life. Their lives were so unique and challenging that it took someone who had the same lifestyle—one of long nights in bunkers and days spent in the mud—to completely understand what it meant to fall in love.

As she pulled down the road that led to the ranch, her headlights bounced as she hit the obstacle course that had been carved into the dirt by the summer winds and fall freezes. The rhythmic back and forth motion of the car comforted her, knowing that the Widow Maker Ranch was protected by the grounds around it. With potholes and ruts this deep, few would venture down their road; the fewer the people, the better.

After Jarrod and Mindy's run-in with the Gray Wolves's—and their leader Bayural's—hit man, they had been trying to stay out of the public eye. That was, until her reentry into society at the trade show. When it came to protecting the innocent, even if it meant coming out of hiding and putting herself in danger, Zoey had been willing to personally take the risk. Their clothing line would make the world a better, safer place. Women like Trish could use their tac line every day and just maybe Zoey could keep someone else from losing a sister.

She checked her rearview mirror one more time. There was a set of headlights behind her, and in the rural Montana countryside they made her nervous. Though she was sure she was overreacting, she pulled her car to the side of the road and let the person behind her pass by. The sedan was blue and had local plates, but she didn't get a good look at the driver.

Not for the first time during the drive, she wished she hadn't gone alone. Mindy had offered to come with her by flying over from Sweden, but Anya— Mindy and Jarrod's adopted daughter—had come down with a cold and it hadn't seemed right for her to leave the girl's side.

Zoey picked up her phone, checking it one more time before she started driving again. As she clicked around her emails and screens, her contacts popped up and front and center was Eli's information.

Was it a sign that she should call him?

It would be nice to hear his voice one more time— maybe it could provide even more closure and she could put her memories back in the past. She stared at the number and her finger trembled over the green phone icon.

If she called him, for a few moments, it could seem like she wasn't completely alone. For those few precious minutes, it would be like she could go back in time and fall into the sweet world of flirty banter and the flutter of excitement that always came with hearing his voice.

No. There was no going back in time, no making things right, and no amount of forgiveness that could right her wrongs.

She clicked off her phone and turned back onto the road. She had to be careful not to lead an attacker back to their hideout.

As she slowed down to avoid another rut in the road, a deer careened out of the darkness, sprinting through her headlights and forcing her to slam on her brakes. The phone went flying in the darkness, flipping to the passenger's side floorboard with a crunching sound. The screen flashed a rainbow shard of colors from the broken screen and died.

The deer stopped on the other side of the road and looked back at her, like it was some messenger of the fates. Bambi killing her phone was one hell of a sign that she was never supposed to get in touch with Eli.

About a half mile from the ranch, the car that had passed her was parked on the side of the road. It looked to be last year's Chevy sedan. As she slowed down to look inside, she noticed that the driver was gone.

There wasn't anything near the car, just pastures

that led up to the ranch house. Beyond that was public forest. So why would they have pulled over here and gotten out of their car? She glanced around, but the light of her headlights illuminated only a few yards of grass peeking out from under their blanket of heavy snow.

Maybe the driver had to relieve themselves, or it was possible that they were getting high.

No one knew where her family was hiding. Her paranoia was nothing more than her guilt rearing its ugly head. It had been a risk by coming out of hiding for the trade show, but it wasn't like she had announced to the world that she was going to be there. It had been quick, and she had tried to fly under the radar before the unveiling.

She couldn't let her anxiety get out of control.

The car was just a car. Besides, her enemies wouldn't be stupid enough to even give her a clue that they were coming.

She took one more look at the Chevy. Her brother's favorite joke came to mind. "How do you find a Chevy owner? They're always sitting in the repair shop."

It was stupid and not really true, but it made her chuckle. More importantly, it relaxed her nerves.

Jarrod and Trevor were already at the main house, but Chad had gone to Sweden to iron things out with the members of the parliament who had finally come around and allowed them to start work at their manufacturing plants. Only a handful of people knew about Chad's whereabouts. She hoped that their being split up would make it harder for any one of them to be located by the people who wanted them all dead. They had been smart and prudent.

We are safe, she told herself.

She peeked back at the car. Still empty.

It's okay. It's human nature to feed into fear-based paranoia, she thought, trying to put a name to her feelings in an attempt to get them under control.

There was a long-standing conversation that circulated throughout law enforcement and military personnel about the differences between paranoia and preparedness. It wasn't crazy or over-the-top to think about the "what ifs" and to take steps to mitigate any dangers. What was crazy was believing that all the "what ifs" were real and out to destroy her.

She considered pulling over and running a scan for any unusual cell phone signals that could be found nearby. But she shrugged off the paranoia and just kept driving.

She sighed, finding more comfort in the vast control that was at her fingertips thanks to technology— her bread and butter.

When it came to tech, she was a badass.

Sitting up a little bit in her seat, she blew off the last bits of fear that wafted through her. The car was nothing.

As she pulled through the gates of the ranch, their newest acquisition, Sir Galahad of Lucktown also known as Sarge, their black gelding, stuck his head over the front fence. He whinnied in greeting as she got out of her car. He threw his head has he pranced around near the fence line.

"Heya, Sarge. Hoping for a cookie, are we?" she said to the horse.

He threw his head again and picked up his pace like he knew exactly what she had said.

"You are spoiled rotten." She chuckled as she walked over to him and ran her hand down the blaze on his forehead. He relaxed under her hand, moving into her touch.

For a new horse, she and the animal had a surprisingly instant bond. It was as if the horse could pick up on the sadness of her losses and the pressure she felt in keeping the family safe.

The house seemed buttoned up and quiet, with the front curtains drawn and the living room light showing through. Everything seemed fine.

It was good to be back at the ranch.

She paused in front of the barn doors and stared up at the chipping white paint of the doorjambs and the hayloft door. The Widow Maker brand was emblazoned above the hayloft door, a broken heart and crooked slash. Oh, the irony. She had come here to move forward, to find safety and to be with the people she loved, but she was constantly reminded of the heartbreak she had suffered with Eli Wayne.

Sarge huffed from the pasture, reminding her that there was no time to waste when it came to getting him his nightly treats.

The barn door squeaked as she slid it partially

open and stepped inside. The place smelled of earth, horse manure and hay. And, as odd at it may have seemed, she loved the scent. It was the aroma of a life well spent, but she wasn't sure if it or the smell of gunpowder brought her more satisfaction.

When they had been young, she and her brothers had come to the Widow Maker to visit their cousin and her family until Gwen's father had died in a haying accident. After that, everything at the ranch and in her cousin's family had seemed to fall into disrepair until Gwen and her mother had finally decided to sell the ranch to Zoey and her brothers. The sale had been somewhat fortuitous. The opportunity had fallen into their laps at the right moment, just when they needed to get their heads down.

Though she had spent time there, it still felt like they were guests. She had hoped that by getting Sarge, it would help with some of that. If nothing else, she could have something that concretely tied her to the place by needing her almost as much as she needed it.

The lights were off in the barn, and she searched around in the dark for the light switch, wishing she had her cell phone to light it up.

It was childish, but one of the things she feared the most was darkness. Perhaps it reminded her too much of death, or perhaps it was just that illogical, primal instinct that evil hid there. There was no way that she would have been out here in the middle of the night looking for food if she hadn't loved Sarge with all of her heart. Evil probably wasn't lurking in the dark, but bears certainly could be.

The horse called to her from the pasture, making her chuckle. "I'm coming, I'm coming… Jeez, you're such a typical dude, always wanting what you want when you want it."

As she groped for the light switch one more time and missed, she gave up hopes of finding it. With the days getting shorter she was going to have to figure out a better system if she was going to be spending any amount of time out here in the barn.

Making her way to the corner of the bench by feel, she came to the end and reached down into what she knew was a bag of horse biscuits. She rolled a few around in her hands and stood up.

Her skin crawled as she stared out into the darkness. "So dark that you couldn't even see your hand in front of your face" wasn't just an adage.

It's nothing. I'm fine. I'm fine.

When was she ever going to get over this fear?

As she moved in the direction of the door, a draft brushed against her cheek.

It's just the wind. Don't be a chicken.

She clenched her eyes shut as her fingers trailed along the rough, splintered edge of the plywood top of the tool bench. She could feel every crack and split in the wood, every sense heightened by her blindness.

Unfortunately, they weren't heightened enough.

A hand wrapped around her mouth from behind.

Before she could even realize what was happening, her body hit the ground. She opened her mouth to speak, but only tasted oats and mud as her assailant pressed her face into the dirt floor.

The Gray Wolves had found them.

They were all going to die.

Grabbing her hands, they wrapped them behind her back high and tight, and drove their knee into her back, pinning her in place. She writhed, hoping to break their grip on her hands, but their grip only tightened—the human equivalent of quicksand.

"Where's Chad?" The voice was tinny and robotic, as though the sound was being emitted from some type of voice-changing tech.

"Get off me," she said, spitting out the debris from her mouth as she spoke.

The knee in her back drove deeper, making pain shoot down her legs. But her assailant said nothing.

She tried to look over her shoulder, hoping to catch a glimpse of something that could help her identify the person on top of her. However, as she moved, a hand grabbed and rolled her face downward. Their touch was rough, likely a man's hand. But from his clean takedown, she doubted that he actually wanted to hurt her.

In this barn, without anyone knowing that she was home, this person could kill her and no one would be the wiser until tomorrow morning. But they were choosing to keep her alive. There was some hope to be found there, but minimal.

Perhaps they were only keeping her alive to question her.

"Where's Chad?" the same robotic voice asked—definitely a phone app.

Why hadn't she run her detection device? She was so stupid sometimes.

Why was it when it came to protecting the ones around her that she was so much more on the ball?

When was she going to learn that the trap of "it won't happen to me" would get her every freaking time?

She squirmed under the person pinning her to the ground. They drove down their knee, making it hard for her to breathe. As she struggled, her body fought for sweet, sweet air. Her squirming turned to thrashing.

She had to fight. There was no way she could surrender. Not just her life was at stake. Her brothers, their fiancées and Anya...they all depended on her.

For a split second, her thoughts moved to Trish's last moments. Had this been what she had been feeling? Incapacitated? Unable to save her own life?

The person holding her down grumbled, and the sound was deep and heavy...that of a man.

"Stop moving," the man said, using the robotic voice app.

It was soul-wrenching that he had taken enough time to type his words out when she had been putting all of her strength into an attempt to break free. It was like she was a grasshopper in the hands of a sadistic boy, a boy holding her down and just watching in sick glee until he was ready to rip off her legs.

She was nothing to this person.

She was powerless.

Chapter Four

Tracking a phone wasn't as hard as a person thought. Zoey knew that just as well as he did, which was probably why she'd turned off her phone. Eli parked his car in the last spot he had gotten her signal. Just down the road was an abandoned car. Had someone picked her up? Was this the car she had been riding in? Had the car been dropped here in a nearly abandoned location in Nowhere, Montana, to mask her real location?

She was smart. No doubt about it.

With the hit out on Chad, it was no wonder that she was taking extreme measures to protect herself and her family.

At the same time, though, did she even know about the hit? It had only come down from the top a matter of hours earlier. He had refused to take the contract, but that didn't mean that other independent operatives hadn't taken on the job.

He should have told her about the contract. He should have gone out of his way to help her. But at the same time, their relationship had been the reason he had been forced to leave his last posting. He couldn't get wrapped up with her again.

Yet, here he was…parked on a nearly deserted country road trying to jump headfirst back into her life.

The mind and the heart were truly different beasts.

If he did find her, he would tell her. He *had* to tell her about the hit on Chad. He didn't know who had taken out the contract on her brother, but from the word on the street, it sounded like they were at odds with a Turkish crime syndicate called the Gray Wolves. The Gray Wolves were responsible for the death of Trish, but why they had continued to come after the Martins was something only Zoey could answer for him.

He looked around for any obvious place she might have gone, but aside from the abandoned car, there was little to go on. He'd made a series of phone calls to friends of his in the FBI and CIA. No one had any knowledge about where Zoey or the rest of the Martins were. One of his friends said that the last known location for Chad had been somewhere in Cairo. However, that had been nearly three months ago and made that information about as useful as an umbrella in a hurricane. He'd thanked them, but he couldn't help feeling that he was wasting time.

He found himself drawn to her. It was inexplicable, but from the moment they had met, they had

had this intrinsic bond. Sometimes it was almost as if they were twin flames, one being able to read the mind of the other, and often that meant that they could also feel for what the other was feeling... And right now, that was terror.

He had to find her. He had to get to her. Even if she never knew that he was there, he had to make sure that she was okay.

Parking his truck, he made his way over to the abandoned car and peered into the window. Inside, mounted on the dashboard, was a detection device. Over the last decade, these devices had become more and more accurate, even to the point where they could pick up exact locations, and pretty much anything tech based. They were a hit man's best friend.

It was odd how many people felt safe behind the anonymity provided by their cell phones. The general public didn't realize how easy it was to hack into any phone call, any phone, any tablet or computer. Anything that put off a signal could be used against them. In many ways, this new generation of tech defense was part of the reason that crimes had started to go down on a national level. For most criminals, technology was above them. Now, it was only highly educated, highly trained tech wizards who could get away with high-level crimes.

Gone were the days of the old-time bank robberies that involved nothing more than a gun and a face mask. Sure, a person could still do it, but the chances were that by the time the perpetrators made it back to their house, the police would already be there waiting for them.

That wasn't to say there weren't petty crimes that went unprosecuted. Hardly, but it wasn't because of law enforcement's inability to get information, rather, it was often that the local officers couldn't afford to handle crimes that didn't warrant it. For example, why spend work hours on a car break-in if an insurance company would pay out for the damage and loss, especially when there was someone else being stabbed three blocks away? Life was irreplaceable, and insurance was there for a reason.

It was part of the reason that, in most large cities, officers didn't even bother responding to misdemeanors. As it stood, the last figure he had heard was that eighty-six percent of robberies went unsolved—and that figure was of those that were reported. He shook his head.

It was no wonder that he had a job. People needed men like him, men who would take a stand against the worst of the worst…a man who was sworn to protect, albeit privately funded by those willing to hire him.

Then again, it wasn't all about the money or he wouldn't have been standing out here in the dark looking for a woman he had sworn to write off again and again.

He stepped back and took a look over the Chevy Malibu. It appeared to be a new car, maybe last year's model. He didn't really track cars; he was more of a truck kind of guy. That was, all except the new Charger Hellcats. Damn, he could really go for one of those. Zero to sixty in 3.4 seconds. In all the right ways, it reminded him of Zoey. Power and strength under the hood, and a body to match, but danger and mayhem was quick on its heels.

He patted his stomach. If he wanted to have even half a chance with her, now or ever, he was going to have to do even more sit-ups.

For her, he wanted to be perfect. Everything she could possibly want and need in a man—at least the man she had said she wanted in the days and nights they had spent together in the field.

He thought about the last time he had seen her. It had been the night everything between them changed... A night from which there may well be no coming back, but damn it...after seeing her in Billings, and seeing her face every time he closed his damn eyes, maybe he had to try. Perhaps they couldn't or wouldn't end up together. His life hadn't been anything like some well-scripted romance, but maybe he could set things right and make sure that everything in her life was okay and she had started to heal—especially since she'd once again lost someone she loved when Trish had died.

He knew how close she had been with Trish. She was the only person that Zoey had ever seemed herself with—besides him. With her sister, she opened up and laughed...really laughed...the kind that made stars dance in her eyes and her cheeks redden.

Zoey was always beautiful, but when she really let herself go and laughed…damn, she was like a sunbeam that could burn away the clouds of anger and loneliness that settled into the valley of his soul.

He found himself staring at the red flickering bar on the Protection 1207i device mounted on the dashboard.

It was possible that she had been tracking him as he was tracking her. He certainly wouldn't have put it outside the range of possibility. And maybe once he had gotten close, she had called "No joy" and bugged out. She was and had always been clever like that, capable of keeping him just close enough and yet just far enough away to keep herself safe.

He peered into the back seat, hoping to see anything that would definitely tie the car to her. There was no hot pink bulletproof dress, no luggage or bags of freebies from a weekend spent at a conference. Hell, there wasn't even a stray straw wrapper.

He pulled the plate number on his phone. It was registered to a shell company out of the Caymans.

Just as he thought. This was the car of someone who knew it was going to be dumped—someone who didn't want the car to be tied to them in any way.

But when he'd worked for STEALTH, they didn't use the Caymans—or Chevys. Either things were changing, or this wasn't actually Zoey's drop car.

His stomach clenched. If it wasn't Zoey's car, then it had to be someone else's…someone who was also tracking her…and it wasn't a wet-behind-the-ears mercenary. They weren't great, leaving the car here and all, but they at least knew the right end of the gun. Which meant that his longtime friends were being hunted, and they were in trouble.

He had heard word of their comings and goings with the Gray Wolves in Turkey, and Trish, but he didn't know the ins and outs of what exactly had happened. Operations like theirs were always kept pretty close to the vest. But, given the fallout, they had to have known that hell was coming in a wave of highly paid killers. Killers without honor—killers that were nothing like him.

He shone his flashlight at the tracks on the dirt road. There were only tire tracks heading down the road and away from the highway. If he acted fast, maybe he could still find whoever had dumped the car.

Hopefully Zoey's phone going black had nothing to do with whoever had left this car.

His mind raced with all the things that could be happening to Zoey right now, ranging from kicking the merc's ass all the way to her tied up and moments away from death somewhere.

He ran back to his truck and, with a spray of gravel, raced off in the direction the tracks were going. Though he had no idea where the road led, or who it would lead to, he had to move. He had to save Zoey. He had to keep her safe.

Using Google Maps, he pulled up a street image of the area around him as he tried, and failed, to weave around the ruts and potholes that littered the dirt road. As he drove, a thin dusting of white snow skittered down from the sky, forcing him to slow down. It was almost as if there were some higher power that wanted to stand in his way, making what he hoped wasn't a life and death situation that much more perilous.

The maps showed a private ranch less than a mile up on his left. Beyond was US Forest Service—public lands.

Crap.

If someone had kidnapped her, or taken her hostage, they very well may have taken her up into the mountains that hugged the valley. If they were up there, and it was starting to snow, it was more than possible he would lose track of them. A matter of a few minutes and a hard snowfall could cover any evidence of her location.

He tried to talk himself down off the ledge of panic. She always complained that he had a way of blowing things out of proportion and being overly dramatic. He could have almost sworn that her favorite thing to say to him had been, "The sky isn't always falling, Eli."

And oh, the look she always gave him when she said it.

He had to see that look again. He had to see *her* again.

The snowfall quickened, coming down in a blizzard of early season white, nearly blinding him thanks to his headlights. As he ascended a hill, his tire connected with a rut, sending his truck to the right and nearly striking the wooden fence post next to the road. He slowed down even though all he wanted to do was hit the gas and not stop until he saw Zoey. Ahead, not too far, was a streetlamp set in the center of a parking lot. It seemed out of place, like a stoic sentinel bravely holding a beacon for weary travelers.

Huddled around the parking area was a barn and, tucked in closer to the mountain, a ranch-style house. This must have been the ranch he had seen on the map. The place was buttoned up; the only sign of life was a deserted pickup parked haphazardly at the edge of the drive, a car behind it and a horse that was skittering back and forth at the fence line.

Zoey had always loved horses. But it seemed like a far stretch that the woman he had known would be settled down enough to buy a horse, live on a ranch and still have time to work with a military-grade weapons manufacturer with worldwide ties to create a line of ballistics gear—and to top it all off, combat Turkish terrorists. Damn, if she was living here, she had one hell of a life.

Unsure whether he should stop or not, he pulled under the light and shut off the engine. Snow landed on his windshield and melted, leaving a smattering of droplets of water as the only reminders of the unique beauty that had fallen from the heavens. It struck him how, in a single instant, something so special could simply be struck from existence.

He tried not to see it as a sign of anything that had to do with Zoey. She was fine. She was going to be all right. He was making something out of nothing.

She was probably inside the ranch house, having a cup of coffee and making plans for her next mission. That was it. He tried to control his thoughts as he stepped outside. The cold bit at his skin and burned his lungs as he drew in a long breath.

There was a rattle of metal on metal and a thud coming from inside the barn. He moved toward the noise. The barn's door was open, but the lamp overhead made the darkness inside the barn even more abyssal.

As he grew near, there was the unmistakable sound of a round being jacked into a gun's chamber.

He rushed toward the sound, pulling his Glock and flicking on his weapon's light, being careful to keep out of sight. He took a moment, scanning the grounds in an attempt to secure the outer perimeter. His only witness was the horse.

Fear threatened to creep in on him as he moved behind the door. He channeled it, forcing it to submit into aggression. Whoever was inside this barn, whatever they were doing, it was going to come down to him or them. Kill or be killed.

His finger moved on the trigger guard, ready. The cool steel against his finger calmed him, centering his focus back to his objective.

He moved around the side of the barn, clicking off his light to stay undetected as he carefully slipped under the pasture fence. Most barns had a Dutch-style door in the back for horses and livestock to come and go. From that vantage, he could enter the scene undetected. As he hustled, the door came into view. Though it was cold, the top of the back door was open. The closed bottom wouldn't provide a great deal of protection in the event of a firefight, but if he played his cards right, things wouldn't go that far. If he was called upon to use deadly force, he felt confident that it would be one and done.

From inside, he heard a woman's muffled groan. "Why?"

He slid open the lock on the bottom of the back door and wound his way inside. The sliding front door let in just enough of the streetlight so that he could see the edge of a silhouette ahead, but remain unseen in the back. He did a quick scan of the stalls as he moved silently to get out of the fatal tunnel created by the barn. The stall just behind the silhouetted man was open, creating the perfect place to hide. He rushed forward, hoping to remain in control and undetected.

As he stepped into the stall, the man in front of him kicked, his foot striking a body that lay on the floor. The woman moaned, the sound wet and gurgling, but muffled by the ground.

He prayed the woman wasn't Zoey—that somehow, he had just come upon a random attack.

"Who sent you?" she asked.

This time, he recognized that voice, *her* voice.

He pointed his gun at the objective's center mass. A light clicked on in the objective's hands. A cell phone. He clicked away, typing something. His face was lit up by the blue light. From where Eli stood, he could make out the dark complexion of the man. He had a tribal-style tattoo that wrapped around his neck and disappeared beneath the dark shirt he wore.

"Where's Chad?" a robotic voice sounded from the man's phone.

It was all the confirmation that Eli needed.

As he pulled the trigger, the bullet ripped from his barrel.

The man didn't even know what hit him.

Chapter Five

Zoey had never been the kind of woman who had hoped for a man to save her, but right now, staring up at Eli's face in the dim light of her attacker's cell phone, she could have kissed him.

It was crazy how one little decision had nearly gotten her killed. That was the last time she would go into a barn without using a light switch.

"Eli," she said, his name dripping from her lips like nectar.

"Is there anyone else?" he asked, moving to clear the rest of the barn. He walked to the front of the barn and flicked on the lights that she had struggled to find.

"I don't think so," she said, lifting her head up from the mud of the ground and glancing around. She moved her hands, which were zipped to her feet behind her back. "Hey." She motioned toward them with her chin.

Taking her unspoken direction, Eli pulled a knife and cut her free.

"Thanks." She sat up, rubbing her wrists where the clear plastic had cut into her flesh. She wiped the dirt from her lips, spitting the remnants of mud and guck from her mouth.

"You okay?" he asked, walking over to her as he holstered his weapon.

She thought about standing to make a point of how strong and unaffected she was by the attack, but her body refused to comply. As she breathed, her ribs ached and her head felt as if it were about to explode. The best she could do was lie. "I'm fine."

Or, at least she would be in a day or two.

He knelt down, coming face-to-face with her as he assessed her well-being.

"Seriously, I'll be okay."

He reached up and his fingers grazed against her cheek where she could feel a lump swelling on her skin. "Your eyes are bloodshot." He looked down to her neck. "You're lucky you broke free of his grasp."

If she was feeling a bit better, she was sure she would have said something about him stating the obvious, but as it was, she could only agree with him. The man's body lay at her feet and, as she glanced in his direction, his body twitched. His head rested on the ground, just feet from where hers had been only moments before. There was a red hole at the center of his forehead and blood was dripping out, twisting down his temple and oozing to the floor where it nearly disappeared in the black dirt and spent hay.

She touched her neck, feeling the hot bruises

where the man's hands had wrapped around her neck and nearly ended her.

"Where're your brothers?" Eli asked, pulling her back to the reality that waited just outside the barn.

His question put her on alert. It was too similar to her attacker's robotic "Where's Chad?"

"What do you mean?" she asked, trying not to sound suspicious.

"Are they inside?" He motioned toward the house.

She shook her head and felt some of the tightness recede from her body as she slipped her hand into Eli's. Squeezing his warm fingers, she tried to force a smile. "I just got here. I don't know about Jarrod and Trevor." She slowly moved to standing with Eli's help.

He brushed her hair out of her face for her. The action was intimate—he was far too close. She let go of his hand and stepped back from him. As much as she loved his touch, it had no place in her life.

"Wait," she said. "What are you doing here?"

He glanced away. "That's not important. What are we going to do with this bastard's body?"

He wasn't getting away from her question that easily, but they did need to focus. The only good news was that, out here in the middle of Mystery, Montana, gunfire wasn't something that was feared. The ranch was close enough to public hunting lands that if anyone heard it, they would write it off as a successful hunter.

Her thoughts turned to the dead guys in the shanty

her brother had found and she grimaced, thinking about how often her family found themselves in need of body removal.

"I would say he could stay in here, but I don't want my horse to spook at the smell." She nudged the body with the toe of her boot.

Eli patted the body down, pulling a wallet from the guy's back pocket. Opening it up, he pulled out a military ID card. "Smitty Foster. Know him?"

She shook her head.

"Is he one of your brothers' friends?"

There was little chance that this bastard wasn't connected with the Gray Wolves—not that they didn't have other enemies. But she wasn't sure she wanted to open up to Eli about everything that was happening in their lives right now. However, the hit man market was a small world. He had known about Trish, which meant it was likely he knew about the Gray Wolves.

"Are you just fishing for information? Or do you really not know what's going on here?" she asked, trying to sound as nonconfrontational as possible. She didn't want to push him away, just get an idea of what they were working with.

He gave her a guilty smile.

"That's what I thought." She wiped off the front of her shirt. "How much do you know?"

He stared at her for a long moment, almost as if he were trying to decide how much information he wanted to give her. His silence ticked her off, but it also drew in memories of what it had been like to be with him day in and day out.

Spontaneity was something she couldn't live without.

"You know about Bayural? About what exactly happened with Trish?" she said, not waiting another second for him to answer.

He nodded. "I got the highlights through the grapevine."

"Uh-huh," she said, holding out her hand and motioning for the guy's wallet so she could give it a quick once-over.

He handed it to her. "Sounds like you ticked off the wrong people."

"You can say that again." She flipped open the wallet. It was definitely bare bones. ID—probably fake—one credit card with the same name as ID, and two hundred dollars in cash. "But we were just doing our jobs."

"When you take out the CIA's trash, you're bound to get your hands dirty."

She closed the wallet and stuffed it into the back pocket of her jeans. "Getting elbow deep in the muck is fine, but it's an entirely different thing when I'm facedown in the crap in my own home."

He stepped closer to her and wiped a bit of mud off her cheek. "If you want, you don't have to face these bastards alone."

"I…" she began, not sure exactly what to say. It was a generous offer and she wanted him to stay, but he had a life of his own, a job that required him, probably a girlfriend everywhere he went, and that was to say nothing of her own life and roadblocks she had carefully put in place when it came to him. "I'm honored that you would offer, but—"

"Stop, Zoey." He put his hands up like he was a street cop controlling traffic—but this was one wreck he couldn't avoid.

"I know what you're going to say," he continued, talking over her feeble attempt to mutter her protests. "I know you. I know what you're thinking. I know that you think my being here is a bad idea. And I agree."

She wasn't sure what hurt worse—the fact that he thought he knew her mind but wasn't trying to make a move on her, or that he agreed it was a bad idea they spend any time together.

"You can't possibly know what I'm thinking." If he could, he would have been running for the hills.

"I think I get the gist. Regardless, though, you need me here."

"I have my brothers," she argued.

"If that's true, where are they now?" He waved around the barn and to the dead man on the floor. "I know you love them, and they love you, but didn't Trish's death show you the limits of what family can *actually* do?"

"How dare you come after my brothers? My team? My sister?" She threw her arms over her chest to keep her hands from striking him. He had no business calling out her family, or what he perceived as their mistakes. Trish's death was a tragedy, and sure, mistakes had been made, but it was none of his business.

He sighed. "I didn't mean it like that. At all. I'm just worried about you." He gave her a cute contrite look that was in direct contradiction to the anger that roiled in her gut. "I just mean that you need protection, someone who is with you through thick or thin. I can do that."

There was no way he was going to take no for an answer, and she wasn't sure that she could even get the word past her lips—not when he had just saved her life.

"Let's just take one day at a time."

A huge smile spread across his wide face, accentuating his chiseled jaw and piercing green eyes. There was a quickening inside of her, as though her body was springing back to life after being so close to death.

"I'll take a day," he said. He crouched down and grabbed the dead guy under the arms.

Unwilling to stand idly by and simply watch as he did the heavy lifting, she took hold of the man's feet and lifted him up. "Where do you think we should put this trash?"

He grunted as he shifted the dead weight in his arms and walked backward toward the open barn door. "Your trunk empty?" he asked, motioning toward her car with his chin.

"It can be." They lugged the body over and dropped him on the ground. The body wheezed as it deflated.

"Huh," Eli said, looking down at the guy. "That's a new one. You ever hear that sound before?"

Though she'd never pulled the trigger and killed a man, thanks to STEALTH she'd heard more than her fair share of dying breaths—just never one postmortem. Bodies did strange things after the soul left them.

"No," she said, opening up the trunk, unloading the boxes from the conference and putting them on the ground next to the body. "What's the weirdest thing you've ever seen with a body?"

He grabbed a box out of the trunk and set it on the ground, taking a moment. "Postmortem hyperthermia. Hands down." He nodded, grabbing a box from her hands. "I was on assignment in Guatemala and came across a woman who had just died of what I think was a drug-induced heart attack. Her daughter had tried to resuscitate her before I arrived on scene. By the time I got there, she'd been down about forty minutes, but she was hot to the touch—hotter than a fever. Like, *crazy* hot."

"Okay, that's weird." She took hold of the dead guy's feet and they flung him into the back of the car. As he landed, the car bounced.

"Yeah, but it got better. The daughter swore that her mother's body had been taken over by a demon. Went into a full panic. I tried to calm her down, but she ended up setting the entire house on fire— mother's body and all."

"Can't say I blame her." She wiped her hands on her dirty jeans, aware that they were precariously close to slipping back into their old ways—bantering with one another, having strange conversations in even stranger circumstances and at the same time enjoying each other's company.

She needed to go back to being pissed off at him. It would make it easier to push him away.

One day at a time.

"I need a shower," she said, trying to avoid spending another second with the man who drew so many feelings and questions. She walked to the barn to make sure there were no obvious signs of a struggle in case anyone stopped by. Thankfully, she appeared to have taken all the damage. She ran her fingers over the spot in her gut where the bullet had struck her only hours before.

Bullet to the chest, nearly strangled to death, beaten and now dealing with her ex—it had been one hell of a day.

Clicking off the barn's light, she walked back to the house with Eli at her side. They were in step with each other as they made their way up onto the porch. It struck her as she grabbed her keys and unlocked the front door that there was no way to hide Eli from her brothers in the light of morning.

They were going to rib her something fierce.

She stopped herself before she opened the door and turned to him. "It may be best if you sleep—"

"In the barn? No. And it's too cold to sleep out

in my truck," he said, cutting her off as though he could really read her mind. "I'll take post outside your bedroom."

"So you can listen to me snore?" she said, opening the front door. He pushed past her, taking point as they entered the house.

"Snore, chat, whatever..." His mischievous grin returned.

She looked away in an attempt to hide her own grin. He couldn't know that he still flustered her. "Don't you have to go to work? Make those bosses happy?"

She could almost hear his grin fade as she brought up one of the many things that could drive them apart, though none were greater than the old hurts that lay between them. "As far as they're concerned, I'm still in Billings at the conference, at least for the next few days."

"And what happens when those few days are over?" She closed and locked the door behind them, then threw her keys into the bowl that sat next to the door.

"Like we said, one day at a time." He walked toward the kitchen like he knew the place. "Besides, I make my own hours."

She raised a brow. When he had worked for them, he was on salary and worked at her side constantly. There was none of the "we'll call you when we need you" freelancer thing. He had been a major part of their team and their lives. It was because of him that they had been forced to change the way they worked. When he left, it became abundantly clear that it was a liability to let anyone outside the family inside their circle at that level…security could be breached best by trust.

There was the sound of him putting water in a teakettle as she walked into the kitchen.

"London fog?" he asked, holding up a box of decaf Earl Grey.

"Sure."

"You're still drinking it every night before you go to bed?" he asked, his back turned to her as he set about working.

It made her squirm that he knew her that intimately. "Um, yeah. Most of the time."

She wasn't sure she should admit it or not. It would have made her feel better to lie and tell him she had changed, that she wasn't the woman he had once known, but aside from making her feel better, it wouldn't have served any purpose. The only thing that had really changed—besides her location—was the need to keep people, and love, at arm's length.

If she could just figure out how to keep Eli close enough to ensure her safety, but far enough away from the danger of falling in love with him all over again.

Chapter Six

Aside from the dead body in the trunk of Zoey's car, things had gone better than he had expected—and he hadn't been forced to tell her anything about what he knew about the situation with Chad. But as he stared at the wall across from her bedroom door, he couldn't help but feel like he had made a mistake in not coming clean.

She needed to know about the contract out on Chad's head.

There was the creaking sound of the floor as she paced around her bedroom. Either she was trying to calm down after the attack or she was working away. Knowing her, it was probably a little bit of both.

It was a relief he had gotten to her in time. A couple of minutes later and who the hell knew what kind of condition she would have been in. She had seemed to think the man only wanted information about her brother, but if that was true, why had he used a voice-cloaking device and attacked her in the dark?

Eli couldn't make sense of why the man had

gone about the attack as he had. If Eli had taken the contract on Chad's head, he wouldn't have dinked around going after his sister in the night; he would have waited, watched and calculated before making any sort of move. The man had been reckless.

By coming here and following Zoey, the man must have been desperate. Perhaps the clock was ticking.

He hadn't gotten the specs on the hit, just that there was a job up for grabs. However, some employers loved to give little bonuses for quick and "accidental" deaths. But it didn't seem like the kind of thing a group like the Gray Wolves would do when ordering such a hit.

But there were a million different conditions and factors he didn't know. Maybe it would have been better if he had taken the contract. At least that way he would know more about the job and what he and Zoey's family could expect. If nothing else, when he decided to tell Zoey the truth, he wouldn't be going to her empty-handed and clueless about what the future was going to bring—other than madness.

He clicked on his phone and contacted his boss, James, at Watch Dog.

ON RECON. SEND ENCRYPTED FILE ON CASE #19807—M8.

In a matter of just a few seconds his boss emailed him the posting. It was the basic details. Chad Martin, date of birth, last known location and a picture.

The photo was grainy and looked like the kind that had been pulled off a surveillance camera. There was a black star at the corner of the picture.

He texted James back:

BLACK STAR =?

This time he waited for James's response, almost as if James had to look it up. After ten minutes he got a text back:

Foreign GOVT assigned

If that were the case, it couldn't have been the Gray Wolves that had put out the contract. Or could it have been? There were several known persons within foreign governments who were also members of militant groups, or funded by them. Perhaps Bayural had paid someone within the Turkish government to put out a hit on Chad. Or, for all he knew, Bayural held a seat in the government.

WHICH ONE? he texted back.

UNKNOWN. MORE INFO ON HIRE.

If he took this job, his employers would expect him to get the kill. They weren't in this business for the familial honor, not like the Martins were. The only thing that mattered to the Watch Dogs was their bottom line. Which meant there was no room for failure if he accepted this contract—if he failed or let his feelings get in the way of finding and killing Chad, they may well put a bead on him. His bosses loved to reiterate that they were only as strong as their weakest link, and they would stop at nothing to be the strongest chain of contractors in the world.

He couldn't rush this decision. But there were no other options to get the information he desperately needed to figure out who had taken out the hit.

He did a quick search on the Gray Wolves and their leader. The public information on the group was sparse: just a few mentions in Turkish papers, Al Jazeera and the BBC. No information on Bayural, or any ties he held in the government or to the prime minister.

Eli didn't know how he would come out of this without hurting himself or someone he loved, but his options were limited. He had to do what he felt was right.

I'LL TAKE THE JOB.

DONE. STANDARD RATES.

He had no problem giving the Watch Dogs their cut so long as he could do what he was really trying to do by taking this job.

Before he clicked off the screen, an email from James landed in his encrypted in-box.

Glancing back at the closed door beside him, he

could make out the sounds of Zoey's pacing. She had to be upset—she was just dealing with it in a different way than he was.

He clicked on the email and took a look at the details spread out before him. Whoever was picking up the tab was serious. As he had assumed, there was a bonus of one million dollars if someone could get the job done within seven days of the posting. According to the date, that was three days ago.

Based on the craziness of the man in her trunk, there was no way they were done dealing with mercenaries who were hungry for a profit.

In addition to the bonus, it looked as though there was a four million flat on taking him down. Five million dollars was a lot of money—his normal jobs paid only low five figures—and then cut the company's commission. Even in his own life that kind of money would make a huge difference. He would never have to raise a gun again. He could retire anywhere. No wonder even the poorly skilled sewer rats had come out to take on the job.

He could see snow still coming down through the window at the end of the hall. Winter was crashing in upon them.

If he did kill Chad, he would probably walk away with more than enough money to buy a place just like this ranch. It was just too bad he knew and liked the man he had just agreed to take out—only time would tell if he would have to pull the trigger or not. The only person he truly wanted to take aim at was the person responsible for putting his friend in the sights.

Though he was paid to think about the "what ifs" in any situation, this time he focused on putting those kinds of thoughts to the back of his mind. For so many years, working with STEALTH, they had always had a focus on the family sticking together. At one point, before things had blown up in his face, he had definitely been part of that family.

Nostalgia beckoned him, but the door to the room beside him opened, and Zoey stuck her head out. "You can't sleep, either?" Her hair was ruffled, as though she had tried to sleep and had wrestled with her pillow. He savored the opportunity to see Zoey in her natural, beautiful state. It reminded him of waking up with her at his side every morning.

"Have a job to do." He slipped his phone into his pocket as his words echoed in the night.

It is just a question of which job, and where my loyalties will stand or fall.

He could feel her gaze upon him, as though she was trying to read between the lines.

"I can leave you alone then," she said, moving to close the bedroom door.

"No," he said with an adamant shake of his head. The last thing he wanted to do was sit out here any longer by himself—especially if she was offering some kind of olive branch. "I was just filling my time while I waited for your bogeyman."

"So, you've come to believe that the man was here for me, not Chad?"

He stood up, his knee popping as he moved.

"Ha," she said, glancing down to his offending appendage and not waiting for him to answer. "Getting older, are we?"

He chuckled. Zoey always had a way of finding his vulnerable spots and aging, especially in this business, was one of them. Killing for a living was a young man's business, and not for someone in their midthirties with a repaired rotator cuff and pins in his ankles that required him to announce their presence anytime he wanted to catch a flight.

"Hey now, I'm not old. I'm just getting more refined," he said, giving her the grin that used to beckon her into his arms.

This time, it didn't work. Instead, she stepped inside the bedroom door. But then she waved for him to follow.

There wasn't much in the way of furniture in her room, just a bed, a dresser and a love seat tucked in the corner. She nodded toward the couch as she walked over to the bed and sat down on the edge on top of a sleeping bag she had unzipped and smoothed into a bedspread—as much as a blue-and-red flannel mummy bag could.

Nervous energy. She'd never been one for caring about the state of her dwelling. They were never in one place long enough to unpack—at least, usually. He remained standing.

"How long have you been here?" he asked.

She cringed as she ran her finger over the zipper of the bag. "Uh, a month or two."

"Going stir-crazy yet?" he asked.

"You have no idea." She pursed her lips, nodding. "Jarrod tried to convince me to stay home, to stay away from the show in Billings, but I couldn't stand staring at these four walls for another second."

"I thought you were working with Mindy on H&K's new line?" he asked.

"Remotely, I'm still working tech with STEALTH. But ever since…well, you know…we've been keeping a low profile." She sucked in a breath. "Which for some, has been easy. Chad has really liked catching up on old basketball highlights." She cocked her eyebrows in feigned annoyance, but he could see the glimmer of love for her brother and his quirks in her eyes.

"He's here, then?" he asked, motioning toward the bedrooms down the hall.

"No," she said. "I'm not sure where he is now, but he was supposed to be coming home from Sweden this week. He had been checking on our manufacturing plant, the one Mindy's father had built near Stockholm." She glanced over at her phone and its broken screen. "I tried to call him when I was driving back from Billings, but it went straight to voice mail. I pulled the info on his phone, but the last data usage was from Sweden two days ago."

Damn, he forgot how good Zoey was to have

around when it came to tech. His new team didn't have anyone that could even compare. She could pinpoint just about anyone on a map at any time, using anything with a digital footprint.

Which reminded him of his phone. All of a sudden it—and the secrets it held—weighed even heavier in his back pocket.

If, even for a moment, she considered him anything less than one hundred percent trustworthy she could probably hack into every device he owned within a matter of hours.

The thought provided him with a new and deeper sense of foreboding.

But if he opened up to her now and told her what he had done, she would probably be forced to turn him out. How could she possibly trust him when five million dollars sat on the table? Zoey would undoubtedly think he was just using her to get close—and he couldn't risk having her flee. If she disappeared, the only time he would likely ever see her again was when her face flashed across the news as a missing person—or worse.

She could glean far more information from the actual post than he could. With all of her skills, she could probably pull everything from the post's initial location and time stamp all the way down to the author's eye color and their DNA sequence.

He *had* to tell her. The chances were okay that he would be able to make her understand why he had taken the job if he told her now, but if he waited…

well, those minimal chances decreased by each passing nanosecond.

He was torn between his promises to his employers and the girl who had broken his heart.

Damn his heart.

"Zoe…" he said with a sigh.

She stopped pacing and looked at him. As though she could read that there was something up on his face, she moved closer. Her scent wafted toward him carrying the floral notes of Marc Jacobs Daisy…her signature scent.

He could feel his pupils dilate as he took her perfume deep into his lungs.

"What's wrong, Eli?" she said, touching his shoulder.

Her fingers were barely touching him, but he could feel them burn into him like they were sparking against his skin. She was the only woman who had ever had that effect on him, but no matter how much he cared for her, he couldn't be sure if those sparks were the kind brought on by lust, love or the magnetism of the forbidden. Knowing his luck, it was probably a combination of them all—but none more than the latter.

"Nothing," he said, drawing himself back as he looked at the hard pink lines of her lips. Damn, what he would give to kiss those lips and to have them both make promises of a future, a future without the pain that no amount of "I'm sorry" could make them forget.

"I know you better than that. Don't lie to me." She stepped even closer, like she was feeling the same pull he was. "If there is anyone in the world that you can be honest with, you know it's me."

Nothing could be further from the truth—but it wasn't because he didn't want to tell her everything. It was just...well, *time* had proven that trusting Zoey Martin with his heart wasn't wise.

He reached up and cupped her cheek in his hand. She drew in a long breath, as though his touch had surprised her. The sound made him drop his fingers from her face and, as they lowered, he grazed his fingertips down the front of her T-shirt, slipping over the hardened surface of her nipple that pressed against the cotton. His body quivered to life as his mind drifted to all the times he had touched that exact place in the past—times he had taken for granted.

"I thought you were here to protect me," she said, her tone as much a question as it was a warning.

They were too close to the past, the future and a place where both of their hearts were threatened. And as she was so kind to remind him, he was there to alleviate the threats to Zoey, not to create more.

He took a step back.

They both needed to sleep. With fresh minds, they could make better decisions. Nighttime was fodder for wicked thoughts and even darker deeds.

"I am." He moved toward the bed, looking back over his shoulder. "You need to get some rest." He pulled back the sheets, fluffed her pillow and motioned for her to get into bed.

"You aren't trying to tell me what to do, are you?" She sounded annoyed, but at the same time there was a lightness to her tone like she found his actions charming.

"Never. I'm smarter than that." He gave her a wicked grin as she walked toward the bed and took off her slippers.

He turned away before she moved between the sheets.

"I'll be just outside your door." He motioned to the hall.

As smart as he thought he was, he would never be gifted enough to see the future—or to know the right answers. For now, the only thing he knew with any certainty was that he was playing with fire.

Chapter Seven

It had been a hell of a long night and she had spent most of it setting up her new burner phone's security until she finally slipped into bed. The little dreaming that she did and that she could remember was all about Eli and being wrapped in his arms. The dreams were just as disconcerting as the reality that he sat just outside of her bedroom door.

They had been close—too close—last night. If he hadn't backed off after he had cupped her cheek, she was sure she would have been putty in his hands.

Her body ached from the refusal of the desires that had pulsed through it like poorly timed techno beats.

She was too old for this kind of feeling. It wasn't like she was eighteen years old and new to fluctuating emotions, no. And it wasn't that she had expected the longing she held for Eli to go away over time, but since they had lost their baby and she had left, she had thought them greatly tempered. How could she want someone so much when there were so many heartbreaking memories that came to mind every time she heard his name?

After getting dressed and checking to make sure that not even a strand of her Barbie-pink hair was out of place, she went to the door. It was no big deal to see him again this morning. He probably hadn't been feeling anything even remotely close to what she had. And, as such, there didn't have to be any awkwardness between them—at least nothing outside of her own head.

She trailed her fingers down the door to the handle just as he had trailed his fingers down her chest last night. Maybe there was something more to his feelings.

She pushed the thoughts away.

Even if there were, it couldn't matter. They had already loved and lost. They had been broken.

The doorknob twisted in her hand as he opened it from the other side.

She cleared her throat and took a step back as the door swung open.

"You don't knock now?" she asked, trying to sound annoyed.

Eli's hair, what little there was of it thanks to his high-and-tight haircut, was ruffled from a night spent pressing his head against the wall. His eyes were bloodshot and there was the scent of morning on him.

"I have to talk to you." His voice was hoarse, as though he hadn't slept at all.

Apparently, her night of tossing and turning was nothing compared to his.

"What?" If he said anything about what had transpired between them last night or in the past, she wasn't sure exactly what she would do. She had to head it off at the pass. "You don't have to worry about last—"

He stopped her with a shake of his head and she couldn't have been more grateful.

"It's about Chad." His words came so fast that they bordered on frenetic.

Her breath caught in her throat. "Did you find him?"

"No." Eli slipped his hand into hers and led her downstairs and to the dining room, away from Jarrod's and Trevor's bedrooms.

He sat her down at the table and brought them each a cup of coffee, but she didn't touch it.

"What's going on, Eli?" She couldn't handle the suspense.

He moved the chair like he was going to sit down beside her, but then he stopped and started pacing. He took a long drink of his coffee as though it could steel his resolve to say whatever it was that he was trying to hold back from her.

"There's a hit out on Chad." His words came out unexpectedly and at a clip.

Numbed by his news, she stared down at the table. She wasn't surprised, but the words sounded hollow, meaningless...as though, if she refused to internalize them, they wouldn't be true.

She took her new burner phone out of her pocket

and turned it on. She dialed Chad's number and put it on speakerphone as she waited for it to ring. The call went straight to voice mail. She was going to tell him to call her, but his mailbox was full.

That wasn't like Chad. Sure, he was busy once in a while and unable to get to his phone, and some people would even call him a bit of a pain in the ass when it came to getting back to them, but he never ignored his work long enough for the mail to be full.

Something was wrong…very wrong.

She closed her eyes and tried to feel Chad, like she had some kind of internal barometer that could read if another of her siblings was alive or dead. No matter how hard she tried, she couldn't feel anything.

Not for the first time in her life, she wished that she had just a little bit of a sixth sense, something like the twin bond that Chad and Trish had sometimes seemed to have…nothing crazy, just enough magic to calm her nerves.

"It's going to be okay, Zoe."

Eli could try to calm her, but he wasn't magic, either. She couldn't lose another sibling. She couldn't lose her brother.

There was only one thing she could do—she had to kill whoever took out the hit on him.

"Who took the job?" she asked.

She wasn't sure, but she could have sworn Eli's face paled.

"It's an open contract." He paused. "Five million."

That was a lot of money—killing a diplomat kind

of money. Not the kind of money that was normally put out on a man like Chad. And an open contract?

Her stomach churned. With an open contract it meant that every jerk and his father would be on the hunt for her brother.

She would have to take down any possible mercenaries one at a time.

Before Eli could say another word, she rushed from the table and sprinted upstairs. She pounded on Trevor's and Jarrod's doors. She couldn't handle this news alone. Not now.

Trevor wasn't going to take this well—he was still having guilt over the loss of Trish. He thought her death was his fault. Though he was taking steps toward forgiving himself, there was no changing the fact that he had watched her die.

Zoey couldn't imagine the state Trevor would be in if they lost Chad, too.

Some losses were too great even for the toughest of men and women.

"Meet me downstairs," she said, calling out to them through their doors.

She hurried back down. Eli was staring into his cup like it could give him a readout on Chad's whereabouts.

"That's not all," he whispered.

"What? What do you mean? Did someone already get to him?" Zoey stopped moving, but her blood pounded in her veins.

"Watch Dog took the contract."

She was breathless. "The company you work for?" she asked, though she knew the answer.

He nodded.

"Which operative is working the hit?" she asked, afraid she already knew.

He looked up at her, pain in his eyes. "I am."

What little was still together inside her shattered. "Get out. Get out of my house."

Eli's face pinched, and he shrank back as though she had punched him in the gut and not the other way around. What in the hell was he thinking?

She had been wrong to think that she could bring Eli back into her life. She should have known that when it came to him, the only thing they were good at was bringing the other to their knees. She had been stupid to think this time would be any different.

He stood before her, unmoving. He had to have heard her tell him to get out. He had to have heard the pain in her voice and the anger that leached through the cracks he'd just reopened in her soul.

Well, if he wasn't going to get the hell out, that didn't mean she couldn't.

She turned to walk out of the room.

Screw him and the horse he rode in on.

She had been his fool too many times.

As she started to leave, Trevor and Jarrod strode into the room. Jarrod's hair was disheveled and matted against the side of his head, uncharacteristic for the stoic and typically well-groomed man it belonged to.

"What's up?" Jarrod asked as Trevor yawned and

wiped the sleep from his eyes. "Wait, Eli? What in the hell are you doing here?" Jarrod shot her a look.

"You talk to him," she said, jabbing a finger at him. "I wash my hands of his nonsense."

She ran upstairs to her room, shoved some toiletries into her purse and grabbed her passport. Though she didn't have a clue where Chad was, it didn't matter. All that was important was getting the hell out of Dodge. If her ex and a hit man had tracked her down and suckered her in, who knew who else was on their way here.

For safe measure, she went to her closet and unlocked her gun safe and pulled out a box of rounds and the M4 she kept there for emergencies.

It had been at least a year since she had actually fired a gun, but she had no doubts about her capabilities as a marksman.

Though her brothers were always the men who pulled the trigger, keeping her at the keyboard, the reality was that she had always been the best shot.

When they had been young, their father had taken them out to the range and soon had them honing their skills at five hundred yards. It had taken her only a day or two at that range before she had dialed her aim into a grouping the size of a nickel.

Yet no matter how accurate her shot, it was another story when it came to taking aim at a man and pulling the trigger. To her, being a woman meant only one less dangling appendage. She was capable of almost anything they could do, except when it came to delivering death. There, she was a world removed from her brothers. They could share a sandwich with a man and then draw and fire upon him with their next breath.

She set the M4 back in the case, and the metal safe made a hollow ring as the gun's butt came down on the cold steel.

It was one thing to order a drone strike on a faceless enemy, but something entirely different when she could look into the eyes of her target.

If only she could order a drone strike on the Gray Wolves.

Her bedroom door swung open and Jarrod walked inside. "Did you actually talk to Eli, or did you just go shooting off at the mouth like you normally do?" Jarrod asked.

Oh, no, he didn't.

She closed the gun safe, rolling the combo wheel to lock it, each action deliberate and slowed by fury.

"You really want to talk to me about going off half-cocked?" She could feel her neck bulge as she seethed. "What, were you down there a full five minutes? I'm sure, in that epic amount of time, Eli could tell you everything... How he just randomly happened to see me in Billings, how he saved me from a killer in the barn and how he was forced into taking a five-million-dollar contract someone put out on Chad? Isn't he just a freaking hero."

"You dropped him, not the other way around. You

don't get to be angry with him about everything that happened."

"This…" she spat, motioning to her face like it was a flashing danger sign. "This has nothing to do with that. This has to do with the fact that he just agreed to kill our brother…and his former friend."

Jarrod laughed, causing another rise in her nearly stroking-out-level blood pressure.

How could Jarrod possibly laugh at a moment like this?

He must have finally noticed how angry he was making her. He stopped laughing. "Dude, Zoey…"

"Don't *dude* me. You are the one being ridiculous right now. It's obvious that Eli is here to manipulate us and get as close to Chad as possible in order to take him out."

Jarrod walked over to her bed and sat down on the edge, just like he had done when she was a child. "I'm not saying that you're not right to be concerned. However, if I were in Eli's shoes, and I needed more information about the contract and how best to close it out, I would have done the same thing. It was smart to agree to the hit." Jarrod rested his hands between his knees. "If he really wanted to kill Chad for the money, do you really think he would have told you about the hit? Eli could have kept it a secret until he had pulled the trigger."

Or he was lulling them with a false sense of safety.

It was smarter that way, keep them in the loop about the hit, make her and her brothers work to keep any other hit man from getting close, while getting closer himself.

There was a whisper from just outside the bedroom door. "Trevor, Eli, if you are going to stand out there eavesdropping you may as well come in and join the damned conversation."

Eli stepped in, but his gaze was firmly planted on the floor. Trevor was close at his heels. They looked like little boys who had been caught with their hands in the cookie jar, but this wasn't some misdeed that she could just shrug off. They were talking about murder.

"Zoey, I promise you that I took the gig with the purest of intentions." Eli finally glanced up at her as he gave her a placating look.

She said nothing.

Trevor stepped beside Jarrod. "I for one think Eli is telling the truth. Now, he could be our greatest source of information. We can watch the posts coming through, maybe even be able to get to Bayural by pinpointing the IP address."

That wasn't exactly how IPs worked, but she didn't bother explaining it to Trevor.

"Actually," Eli started, "I don't think that this job was posted by a Gray Wolf. According to my info, the contract was put out by a foreign government, not an individual."

She huffed. "Turkey, I am sure. Bayural has his hands in every diplomat's pockets."

Eli shook his head and sent her an apologetic

glance. "No… I just got word that it was put out by someone in Algeria."

"Algeria?" she asked, surprised. There was a collection of countries that Bayural and the Gray Wolves could have maybe been working with, but Algeria didn't seem like the kind of country that would be on that list. They had nothing, at least that she could think of, that would be gained by allying themselves with a terrorist group and then doing their dirty work.

"From the way I see it, it doesn't make a whole hell of a lot of sense, but at least we have a bit of information to start working off. It's better than nothing." Eli gave her self-effacing smile.

Though she was still miffed, Eli was proving to be more helpful than she cared to admit. Without him, they'd have no knowledge of what was coming down from behind the enemy's lines.

"Eli has a point. Good work, man," Jarrod said with a slap to his back, as though he was just another of her brothers. He turned to Eli. "But what was that talk about a dead body?"

Chapter Eight

He wasn't even close to being out of the woods when it came to getting back into Zoey's good graces. Though Jarrod had managed to get a pass from Zoey, from the way she looked at him, she still clearly thought he was trying to make a move against the family.

He was going to have to prove that he was someone she could trust. Even if it took him his whole life, he would prove to her that he wasn't the man she thought she knew.

Jarrod looked at him, waiting for him to answer for the dead man in Zoey's trunk.

"What can I say, the dude picked the wrong woman to come after." Eli smirked as he gave an appreciative nod in Zoey's direction.

"Do you think this is going to be a continuing problem?" Jarrod asked. He was always the one taking charge.

Eli nodded. "Unfortunately, I think it's possible. I believe he was working some of the same angles as I was, scoping out places your family would be tempted to go. After hearing whispers about you guys getting into large-scale gun manufacturing in Sweden, I narrowed it down to just a few places you would likely make a public appearance."

Zoey opened her mouth like she was going to speak, but quickly closed it.

"If I can figure out your family's possible movements, then others will, as well."

Zoey stormed off toward the door, grabbing her purse. "We have to get out of here." She looked to Trevor and Jarrod. "Where are Mindy and Sabrina?"

"They haven't gotten back from their trip to H&K. And they have Anya with them." Trevor took out his phone and tapped on the screen like he was hoping to hear from his fiancée at any moment.

"When do they touch down?" Eli asked.

Trevor looked up from his phone. "They're supposed to be arriving into Missoula at about five thirty tomorrow. They are leaving Stockholm this afternoon. Coming through London."

Eli nodded. "Tell them to stay in place."

"Have they seen Chad?" Zoey sounded like a frantic mother.

Jarrod scowled. The unspoken tension between Jarrod and his sister was nearly palpable.

Eli wasn't sure what the source of mixed feelings was between them, but he knew well enough to let it alone. The Martin crew was a special breed—

loyal to the death, but often found nipping at each other's ankles.

On more than one occasion, when he had first taken the job with their team, he had found himself at the center of one of their feuds. Zoey and Jarrod had been discussing which scope covers to buy and use for their growing team. Their discussion had quickly turned into a near yelling match. The only reason it hadn't was that Trish had stepped in and acted as their ballast.

It struck him that perhaps that was what was going on; the Martin equilibrium was thrown off due to Trish's death.

"No one has spoken to Chad in three days." Trevor's face pinched.

Even for a Martin outsider that was concerning. "That was when the contract went live," Eli said. "The good news is that the contract is still active. As of now, he is still considered to be alive." He tried to sound hopeful though everyone in that room knew just as well as he did that sometimes it took several weeks for a contract to be taken down after being completed.

"We need to find him," Jarrod said.

Zoey gave him an irritated look. "Thanks for joining the party."

Jarrod ignored her. "Did you check his credit card activity yet?"

Zoey opened and then closed her mouth. She shook her head. "I was hoping to hear that one of you had spoken to him."

She looked a bit crestfallen that Jarrod had gotten the better of her.

"You take care of looking into his paper trail and Trevor and I will take care of your friend out in the trunk and his Chevy." Jarrod strode to the door as he worked away on his phone, likely calling in their disposal team. "We'll take your car. If you need to go anywhere you'll have to make amends with Eli."

Jarrod gave him a sly grin.

He had always gotten along well with Jarrod, which had sometimes irritated Zoey when they didn't see eye to eye, but the brother's attempt to help further their reconciliation surprised him. It made him wonder if Jarrod knew something he didn't. Perhaps he advocated their getting back together…or perhaps he just liked having an extra set of hands around in this emergency.

Or maybe he didn't trust him and the best way to keep tabs on him was by keeping him at heel.

He liked his first thought the best.

As the brothers left him alone with Zoey, there was a long moment before either of them spoke. When she sighed, he was afraid she was about to let him have it. He certainly deserved it. Instead, she surprised him. "Sorry about that display with Jarrod. Some things never change."

And from what he saw, things had only gotten worse.

"You're fine. You know how things are with my family. I'm in no place to judge."

"You still don't speak to them?" The look in her eyes moved a click closer to pity.

"No." He shouldn't have brought his family up. They, and the nonsense they brought with them, was one topic he would rather leave buried in the past. "And what Jarrod said about amends, don't worry about it. Whatever you're feeling toward me, it's justified. I should've let you in on the truth from the very beginning, I just didn't know how to go about it. With everything that happened between us, I just wanted to get everything right."

She dropped her purse to the floor and walked over to him. Putting her hands on his face, she looked him in the eyes. "I'm the one who should say sorry. I know I can be hard to put up with, and I can get things so wrong sometimes—especially when it comes to relationships."

Her fingers were warm on his cheeks, and she ran her thumbs over the stubble that had accumulated over the last day.

"I shouldn't have just left you," she said. "I just didn't know where I wanted things to go with us. We were getting so close to having our own family. I guess it scared me. And then when…"

"We lost the baby…" The words threatened to choke him as he finished her sentence. "It hurt me just as much as it hurt you. I hope you know that I've thought of you every day we were apart. And I don't expect us to get to the place we were ever again, but I'm hoping we can be friends."

"Is that why you're *really* here?" Her hands moved to his shoulders and then drifted down his arms.

It was one of the many reasons, and though he wanted to tell her he had spent almost every waking hour dreaming of her and what the future could have been, he said nothing. It took Zoey so much to open up to him that he didn't want to make this about himself. She was the one who really mattered.

He leaned in to kiss her, the movement instinctual. Just before their lips met, he realized what he was doing, and turned his face so his lips brushed against her cheek. He let them rest there for a second too long, as he took in a long breath of her.

She stepped back, but her hand drifted into his and she squeezed his fingers. "I'm glad you're back, Eli. And I think you're right… I don't think we're ever going to get to the same place again. I was never meant to have children."

There was a finality in her words, and they tore at his heart.

She let go of his hand, moved across the room and grabbed her computer out of her bag. She clicked it on.

After about an hour of them working side-by-side, he excused himself and went to get two fresh cups of coffee as she continued to work. Her brothers, and the car in the driveway, were gone.

As he moved around the house, he couldn't deny that this place somehow felt like home, though he had never been here before. Perhaps it was just that she was here.

He took a sip of his coffee as he stood in front of the bay windows and stared outside. He could live here, surrounded by the wilderness and watching the snow as it drifted down from the sky. There was no traffic, no crowds, no dust storms on the horizon, and no sand wedged into every crevice of his body. If there had been a crackling fire in the fireplace, it could've been the quintessential Montana dream.

There was a creak in the floorboard behind him, and as he turned there was the blur of an object coming at his head. He dropped down, dodging the impact. The coffee cups he had been holding shattered as he let them fall from his grip. Hot coffee spread across the floor and splattered upon his hands, but he didn't feel any pain.

A man lunged toward him, a shotgun in his hands. He racked a shell into the gun's chamber with a loud metallic crack. Eli couldn't make out the man's features, but he looked to be about six foot five and pushing three bills.

It was a wonder the man had tried to be stealthy by swinging the gun instead of shooting him. Eli had been lucky.

The giant aimed from his hip as his finger moved to the trigger. Eli threw himself toward the couch. He rolled behind it as the gun boomed and a spray of BBs hit the corner where he had just been. Tufts of the cushions flew up into the air, making it look as though snow was falling inside of the room.

Eli reached behind his back, looking for his Glock. His fingers wrapped around the gun's handle and he pulled it from his holster. There was already a round in the chamber. All he had to do was get a bead on this dude without getting hit.

He thought of Zoey upstairs. What if there were more than one hit man this time? Even if not, Zoey would be rushing down here at the sound of the gun's blast. He needed to make quick work of this guy to make sure she didn't find herself in harm's way. He had to protect her.

He belly crawled to the edge of the couch where a round had just struck. The man's footsteps pounded against the wood floor as he rushed toward him and racked another round into the chamber. The giant had only two more shots before the magazine was empty.

Eli took a breath as he rolled around the corner and took aim at the man's center mass. He pulled the trigger. The shot rang out and struck true. The giant stepped back, shock on his face as his left hand dropped from his shotgun and he looked down at his chest. Blood seeped through his gray T-shirt.

"What in the hell?" the man said, like he was surprised any bullet had ever found him.

Eli fired again, hoping this time to bring the man to the ground and eliminate the threat. The bullet struck millimeters to the left of his original shot.

The giant took another step, obscenities streaming from his mouth like a spray of spittle.

He still didn't fall to his knees. The man raised his shotgun. Eli dodged behind the couch again, hoping this time he would still have enough cushion to provide cover. The giant fired off another shot in Eli's direction. A BB struck Eli's shoulder, embedding in his skin. He touched the spot—it was already bleeding.

The couch was one piss-poor excuse for a barricade, and it wouldn't withstand another shot. He held no doubt that the man had another firearm with him, probably something very similar to his own.

He crawled toward the other corner, hoping against all hope that he would get there in time enough to surprise his attacker and go for the one shot he knew would take the man down.

As he neared the far corner of the couch, he moved to round it as he was met with the sound of the man racking a round into the chamber. It was now or never—he lunged his body around the corner and took aim, the motion instinctual.

The giant pulled the trigger of the shotgun as Eli's round ripped through him. The shotgun's recoil went unchecked by the man's strength, sending the BBs astray and just above Eli's head, barely missing him and striking the wall behind him with a cascade of dull thuds.

The man crumpled and collapsed onto the ground.

Eli got up. Standing at the top of the stairs, looking down at them with a gun in her shaking hands, was Zoey.

He motioned for her to stay put as he moved closer to the man, keeping a bead on him in case he wasn't dead. Yet, as he drew nearer, he could make out the round edge of a bullet wound between the guy's eyes.

There was the sound of a gun hitting the floor as Zoey rushed down the stairs, straight to him, "Are you okay?" she asked, looking him over. "You're bleeding. Do you need to go to the hospital?"

He glanced down to the blood spot at his shoulder. "It's nothing. I'll be fine."

He shoved his gun back into its holster. Zoey stepped over and looked at the dead man lying in the middle of her family's living room.

She was the one who wasn't okay. None of her family was going to be okay. They had to act. Fast.

This was no longer a game of rekindling old flames; it had swiftly become a battle of kill or be killed.

Chapter Nine

Zoey's hands trembled as the adrenaline worked its way out of her system. The residue of fear mixed with the elixir of relief made a sickening sense of nausea rise up from her core. She had nearly pulled the trigger. In fact, it could have been her bullet that had ripped through his skull.

Blood pooled on her mother and father's Oriental rug. It had been in the family for years and now it was destroyed. The cranberry-colored liquid seeped into the ochre strands as the reality of what she had almost done crept deeper into her core.

She could have been a murderer.

"We have to get out of here," Eli said. "My truck is just down the road. We can go anywhere you want, but you can't stay in this house until this thing with Chad is under control."

Though she heard the words coming out of Eli's mouth, she couldn't process them. It was as if he was talking to her through a tin can, the sound ringing and otherworldly.

Her finger twitched as she stared at the man on the floor.

All she had thought about was that if she didn't pull the trigger Eli was going to die and he would be gone from her life forever.

And yet, she had failed to be brave enough to take the shot. The world started to spin.

Eli moved closer to her, wrapping her in his arms as though he could sense she was about to go down

"You're okay. It's going to be okay," he said, moving her toward the nearly destroyed couch and making her sit down.

This couch had been all that stood between him and death.

What if she had come downstairs instead of Eli? In the barn, Eli was the only reason that she had even survived. In a sense, he had saved her twice.

It was like they were back in a war zone, except this was the place her family had intended on making their home. Now, BBs were lodged in the couch and there was blood spatter on the wall behind the attacker. Her home had become a death zone.

"Just breathe," Eli said as another wave of lightheadedness came over her.

Her hands were still trembling in her lap and she was shaking her legs, restless.

It was okay. Everything was going to be fine.

Eli was right. She couldn't deal with the emotions that came with what had just happened. She had to keep moving. If they fell under attack once again, the odds might not play out in their favor.

They had to get the hell out of this shooting gallery.

She stood up. Her knees were weak and threatened to buckle beneath her, but she summoned as much strength as she could to take a step. As she moved, it reminded her of the day she lost the baby, leaving them alone in the world. Here she was again, her world threatening to collapse. The only thing she could do was find the courage to keep moving forward, just as she had done before.

Thankfully, Eli was here. This time, she had to stay. She couldn't just walk out and deal with this on her own as she had done before. Though things would be different between them, and they weren't likely to find their way back into a serious relationship, that didn't mean they couldn't be each other's greatest ally.

It took them only a few minutes for her to grab her go-bag and bug out, leaving the dead guy on the floor. No one would find him. She called her brothers as they walked down the road to Eli's truck. Being in killers' crosshairs was proving to be much harder than she had ever assumed. If things ever got back to normal, she would never complain about sitting behind a computer again. She would take carpal tunnel over a bullet any day.

Trevor answered his phone on the second ring. "It's done," he said, not waiting for her to speak.

"There's more trash to take out. I left it in the living room for you." Her footsteps crunched in the fresh snow as she walked to the passenger side of Eli's Dodge pickup. "I recommend leaving it there for now. It's too hot in the house for any of us."

There was a long pause on the other end of the line as Trevor must have been deciphering her code. Now more than ever, it seemed that everything in their lives was coming under scrutiny. Nothing they did or said over open communication lines was safe. They were being monitored.

"Understood."

"We need to enact COBRA," she said, using the code word for going underground. All their cell phones would be destroyed, along with any other forms of communication technology that could be tracked back to them.

In a sense, they would all be going dark. It was likely what Chad had done and why he had been so impossible to pin down—if he were still alive.

It was what they had all been trained to do in an event like this—stay low, seek shelter.

Unfortunately, with their house no longer available, there were no safe zones. Thankfully, they had protocol for this type of event. Each of them had bags stashed in various locations with devices with state-of-the-art encryption—she had taken care of all the phones and tablets herself.

She grabbed her go-bag and rifled through it. It had everything she needed to get away. As it was, however, they wouldn't have access to their regular email accounts—they were already known and the information within them lay in the hands of their hunters. And, if they accessed their accounts through their new phones, it would be only a few hours before their locations would once again be known.

They would have to be extremely careful. There were nearly a million ways they could be tracked down if any one of them accidently clicked on the wrong button.

The other end of the line was muffled as Trevor must've said something to Jarrod. After a moment, he returned to the phone. "Done."

"In the meantime, look into our new friend in the government. I will expect to hear from you soon."

Trevor grunted in acknowledgment on the other end of the line. When the line went dead, she took out the battery from her phone and snapped the SIM card, then threw them all out the window toward the pasture.

When they were well away from the ranch, she would turn on her other equipment, but not yet, not with possible enemies lurking around every corner.

Eli started the truck, letting it roar to life. He kicked up bits of snow and gravel as he took off.

She wasn't sure whether she should ask him where they were going or just let him lead the way. There was enough information out there that if someone wanted to find her, it may not have taken too much digging. But no one would guess she would leave her heart and safety in the hands of her ex—only a madwoman would do something so stupid...or someone incredibly desperate.

The midday sun bounced off the front window just as they crossed over the Montana-Idaho line. They were stuck behind a line of truckers ascending the pass. There always had to be that one driver who found fault in the others around them and decided to pass the line of cars, only to find that the left lane was snow packed and icy and far more treacherous than they had anticipated. In a way it acted like a metaphor for her life—just when she thought she was ready to take control of the world around her, her hubris caught up with her.

She should never have gone to Billings. Everyone had warned her to stay home and out of the limelight. She had been an idiot and fallen into the trap of complacency. She should've known better.

As they crested the hill and made their way deeper into the panhandle of Idaho, she turned on her phone. Eli gave her a glance, like he wasn't sure whether or not it was safe for her to be doing so.

"Even if people are tracking phones, if they find the signal they won't think anything of it. This line is assigned to an alias. Even if they take the time to look it up, the findings won't go anywhere. We are safe, at least for now." She didn't tell him the part about how she didn't dare to delve too deep into the internet.

She wanted to reach out to her brothers to make sure they were okay, and to see where they were headed, but she didn't dare just yet.

"I'm coming to learn that safe is relative," Eli said.

"Why would you say that?" She clicked off the screen after making sure the phone was fully charged.

"I shot that man twice, center mass. Nothing happened. He wasn't wearing standard body armor, but the bullets didn't penetrate. It was like he was wearing something similar to your dress at the trade show." Eli gave her an appraising glance like he was questioning her culpability in the attack.

"If you're implying that I gave this man bullet-proof clothing so he could break in, shoot up my house and try to kill us, then you are crazy." Something like that wouldn't even make sense. "I thought by now you would know you can trust me, and I thought I could trust you. Let's not take two steps back. Not now. The only way we are going to make it out of this, or at least the only way I will make it out of this, is if we stick together. Eli, I can't do this alone." She could hear the pleading edge to her voice, but as she spoke she didn't try to muffle it.

"I know." He sat in silence for a long moment, staring at the road. "I just wanted to make sure that you weren't somehow involved in this."

"I know it's been a long time since we were to-gether, but I'd like to say that I've changed for the better." She felt exhaustion seep into her core at having to fight to prove who she was. "I'm not entirely evil."

"Well, now I know you're telling me the truth—you're still a little bit evil. If you tried to tell me you were a saint…we'd be having a very different conversation," he said with a laugh. "In fact, that bit of duality is part of the reason I have always thought of you as someone special—you're not like everyone else. You say what you mean, even if it's something you know people aren't going to want to hear, and you are unapologetically yourself."

She laughed. He hit the nail on the head with that one. Most people wouldn't consider those strengths, but rather character defects. More than one of her exes had chewed her out for embarrassing them by saying the wrong thing to the wrong person.

Luckily, she had never let the criticism of others change her. She was unstoppable. But Eli's compliments made her uncomfortable, like a jacket that brought her warmth but rested too heavy on her shoulders.

It was easier to shrug off criticism than it was to accept praise.

"You're only saying that because you saw me in that pink dress," she teased, hoping to ease some of the pressure. "I saw the way you looked at me up there."

She could have sworn that she saw a blush rise on his cheeks, but it was something so rare on him that she couldn't be sure it wasn't simply a trick of the light.

"Ha! Is that how you respond to a compliment, by searching for another?" he joked. "If that's what you want, well… I have to admit—"

"Wait," she said, interrupting him as a thought

crossed her mind. "Mindy had her marketing team give samples of our new line to a select group of foreign leaders."

"Algerian leaders?"

She shrugged. "I have no idea who we ended up sending them to."

"Looks like we're going to need to give Mindy a call," he said as he took the off-ramp at the first exit in Coeur d'Alene.

She moved to make the call, but stopped herself. It was more than likely that there were people out there who were monitoring Mindy's phone calls. She had to use another number. Using an app, she grabbed a number assigned to a man out of Newark. It would do the trick. If their enemies went digging they would be looking on the other side of the country.

She dialed, hoping Mindy would pick up even though she wouldn't recognize the man's name or number.

After a couple of rounds of ring backs of "Woman Up" by Meghan Trainor, Mindy picked up the phone. "Hello, this is Mindy. How can I help you?" she asked, like she was a well-seasoned receptionist instead of the owner of a multimillion-dollar company.

"It's me," Zoey said, hoping she would recognize her voice. "Are you holed up?"

She could almost hear the relief in Mindy's sigh. "Yes, we're in—"

"Don't tell me. But you are safe?"

"Yes, I'm with Sabrina. Everything is fine. Are Trevor and Jarrod okay?"

"They're good," Zoey said, hoping that she was right. "I'm calling about the samples we sent out for the new Monster Wear. Do you have a list of people we shipped samples to?"

Mindy paused. "I think so."

"Perfect." Zoey gave Eli a thumbs-up. For once, the stars were almost aligning.

There was a moment of quiet as Mindy must have been scrolling through her phone. "Okay, it looks like we sent out samples to about thirty heads of state."

"Did you send any to Algeria?"

Mindy made a noise as though she were sucking on her teeth as she read over her list. "Yeah, looks like we sent three white T-shirts and two pairs of Monster Wear jeans to the prime minister."

There was no way that the man in the living room was the prime minister of Algeria, that much she knew for sure. "Did you send the white T-shirts to anyone else?"

"Looks like members of the Swedish parliament, but no one else. Why?"

Was someone in the Swedish government coming after them and trying to make it look like it was an Algerian hit? Zoey's thoughts moved to a few months ago and the nerve agent attack on Jarrod and Mindy.

"Do you still have enemies in Sweden?" Zoey asked.

"No, I don't think so. We've been well received

after…well, everything. In fact, most have been apologetic about the whole incident."

That didn't mean they were in the clear when it came to Swedish ties, but she had to hope that this case was going to be more cut and dry than the last. "Good, but let me know if you think of anyone or anything that strikes you as odd," Zoey said, trying to make sense of all the thoughts that were flooding her mind.

"Actually, did you make a wire transfer out of our corporate expense account?" Mindy asked.

"No, why?"

"It looks as though someone transferred $500,226.23 from our account. Do I need to flag it at our bank?" Mindy sounded a bit breathless. "Do you think someone stole it?"

That was a lot of money. And an odd amount. Who transferred twenty-three cents in change? "Have you looked into it at all?"

"Looks like it was transferred to a bank just outside of Barcelona. A town called Sitges. It was processed to be taken out in cash."

"Do you know who picked it up? Their name?"

"John Smith." Mindy huffed. "I was hoping you had something to do with it."

"I'll take a look at it. For now, have the bank put a hold on all accounts not vital for handling the daily expenses. Only give access to our VP of finance and you and me. We need to stop any leaks before we lose everything."

Chapter Ten

Five hundred thousand. That was more than the average American's initial mortgage loan. For some, it would be enough to live off for the rest of their lives. And yet, H&K had enough liquid resources to transfer that kind of money without anyone panicking. Eli shook his head.

Now the five-million-dollar bounty on Chad's head made sense. Everyone around him was rolling in money.

He would never know what a life like that was like. Sure, he had enough to pay his bills and never have to worry about where his next meal would come from, but he couldn't imagine not being overly concerned about a missing five hundred grand from his bank account.

"What do you think is going on?" Eli asked.

Zoey was staring down at her phone. Maybe she wasn't taking the loss of that kind of money as flippantly as he thought she had been.

"Are you okay?" he asked, when she refused to answer.

She pointed in the direction of a Starbucks. "I'm going to need a coffee."

Yep, she wasn't taking this well. His body relaxed a little bit as she returned to the land of normal Americans who lived on a budget. He loved the idea of her being successful and doing well with her family and their businesses, but he wasn't sure that he could be with a woman who was a magnate—he would always feel completely out of her league. He wanted to be an equal partner in any relationship, and that wasn't limited to fiscal matters.

He pulled into the Starbucks and parked. "Want a caramel macchiato, two pumps of hazelnut?"

She smiled. "We can go in together. You still like your coffee so dark and bold that it can hold the spoon up, right?"

He laughed. "A lot can change, but as far as I'm concerned there is only one way to take coffee and that's it."

She rolled her eyes in feigned exasperation. Before getting out, she turned around and grabbed a tablet from out of her bag. She turned it on and connected into the Wi-Fi.

"Seriously, open Wi-Fi? You're good with that?" Eli was surprised.

"Often, it's best if we just hide in plain sight." She gave him a sly grin as she took a beanie-style hat out of her bag and slipped it over her pink hair.

She handed him a baseball cap. "But I would hate to be too obvious."

He slipped on the hat, aware that it would keep him anonymous in the coffee shop's cameras.

Inside, the place smelled like pumpkin spice lattes, hopeful writers and daring entrepreneurs. He loved it.

After ordering the coffees and making their way to a private table, Zoey turned her tablet back on and set to work. He watched her as she frowned and nibbled on her lip. She had always made the same face when she was concentrating and working hard. He had nearly forgotten how beautiful it looked.

There was a strand of pink hair poking out from under her gray hat and it sat at the center of her forehead. Each time she huffed, the little hair would flutter up and down like a frustrated mother's arms.

Finally, she smiled and looked up at him with a vindicated look in her eyes. "I think I got it."

"What?"

She moved so he could see her screen. "It looks as though the money was transferred to the BBVA bank in Sitges. About six hours ago, a man came in and picked it up, one John Smith." She clicked on a few buttons and pulled up the bank's security camera feed.

"Did you seriously hack into a bank's mainframe on public Wi-Fi in a matter of minutes?" he asked, both impressed and uncomfortable. Out of some intrinsic fear, he looked over his shoulder, as if one of the other people in the shop could see what they were up to.

She put her finger to her mouth, motioning for him to be quiet. "This is the best place to do it. Now watch," she said, pointing to the screen.

The video was of the entire bank's lobby, and though the area wasn't large, the size of the room made it seem as though they were zoomed out quite a bit. A man walked in from the street wearing a dark tan jacket and a wide-brimmed hat. He made his way up to the teller. A few moments later, a woman walked into the bank and stood behind him.

Though she was never closer than five feet from him, the way she moved made Eli wonder if they were together. The teller disappeared from the screen for a moment, then returned and started talking to the man.

Though they could not hear what the people were saying, they watched as the man produced an ID. The teller nodded, seeming appeased. The teller walked out of the frame and quickly returned carrying a small stack of wrapped euros.

Perhaps there was an odd number in the transfer because of the exchange rate. And there might have been some sort of fee for sending the money, but he wasn't sure.

The manager turned toward the cash drawer and pulled out a random selection of coins. Eli shook his head. Maybe his theory was wrong. Maybe this had nothing to do with exchange rates and fees. Rather, there was something more to the odd number of transferred monies. But what?

The man in the video turned, and looked straight up at the cameras. As he moved, the woman behind him jabbed him in the ribs, forcing him to look down. They took the money and quickly left.

Zoey turned off the video. "Did you see that?"

Of course he had seen it, it was a video. But it didn't seem like the time to be a smart-ass. "Which part?"

"That." Zoey turned to her tablet and skipped back to the moment the man looked up at the camera. "There... That's Chad. He's alive." There was palpable relief in her tone.

"Good." Hopefully Chad would stay that way. Eli squinted in an attempt to make out the man's face just a little bit better. "Who's the woman?"

"I have no idea," she said, moving closer to the screen like she was trying to see some tiny detail that could possibly give away the woman's identity.

"Has Chad been dating anyone?"

"No. At least not that I know of. But who knows what he's up to these days. When it comes to that kind of thing, he normally keeps to himself."

He and Chad had never been super close. They had never worked a job together, but it wasn't because they had a difference of opinion or didn't like one another. It was just that Chad was normally the man they sent to be a bull in a china shop and Eli was the man they sent in to make a death look natural.

Needless to say, they had different methods when it came to doing their jobs.

After finishing their coffees, they made their way back out to the truck. With the door closed, he turned to her. "Let's have Mindy and Sabrina look into the Swedish and Algerian ties—maybe they can get info about the officials there and find out if anyone has a grudge or reason to want to align themselves with the Gray Wolves."

She let out a long exhale. "Do you think we should go to Spain?"

"It's as good a place as anywhere. As far as we know, no one else has spotted Chad. If we get there before anyone else does, we have a chance of getting him to safety."

"Where would *safety* be, exactly?" she asked, sounding tired.

He couldn't answer her with any level of honesty. Right now, her family's world was upside down, and tangentially his was as well since he had allied himself with them. "The Gray Wolves can't hunt you forever." Even as he spoke, he heard the lie in his words.

"I'd like to think that, but so far that has yet to be true," she said with a haggard look.

He should have stayed quiet.

Calling Mindy, Zoey told her the plan. It took only a few minutes, and though Zoey hadn't heard from Trevor and Jarrod yet, it would be only a matter of time until she did—as long as they were safe. He had to assume they were all right. At the thought, he could feel his blood pressure rise, putting pressure on his eyes. The last thing they needed was for all of the brothers to be one step away from being murdered, but it seemed like that was exactly where they were.

He had to stop playing out the worst-case scenarios in his head. This wasn't getting them anywhere.

"You have your passport?" he asked.

"Which one?" she said, motioning toward the back.

This was going to be one hell of an adventure— hopefully, they would both make it out alive.

Chapter Eleven

There was a private jet waiting for them on the tarmac in Spokane. They drove out to the plane and made their way in with a simple nod to the pilot and the staff.

Thankfully, there had been no snow on this side of the continental divide and it appeared they would have an easy flight to Spain.

Back in the day, when they were dating, Eli would have undoubtedly made some stupid joke about joining the mile-high club. Instead, once he was settled, he sat in near silence across the aisle from her. He sipped on a tumbler of Kentucky Bourbon and flipped through a magazine. Somehow, they had gone from lovers, to enemies, to allies, to an old married couple in just a few days.

Oh, how time flew.

As the sun began to set as they headed east, it lit up the cabin and a shaft of bright pink light was reflected against his cheek, making his stubble stand out. She had always loved that look on him and it harkened to a time when they had been comfortable enough to really let the other see them—warts and all.

She thought of herself; he may have had a wart or two, but she was the one who was weighed down by them.

He flipped the page of the magazine.

"Are you going to stare at me the entire flight?" he asked, giving her a sly grin.

Without missing a beat, though she was embarrassed at being caught staring, she replied, "I was just wondering how long you were going to go before you noticed the booger hanging out of your nose." She laughed, mocking him by playfully wiping at her own.

He instinctively rubbed at his nose, finding nothing. He smirked. "You think you're cute, don't you?"

She laughed, the noise coming from deep in her belly. As the sound escaped her, she caught herself, afraid that by really truly laughing she was minimizing the situation in which they found themselves. As she thought about it, she realized this was the first time she had really laughed in months—since Trish's death.

"What are you reading?" she asked.

"You know, you didn't have to sit all the way over there." He nudged his chin toward her. "Why don't you scoot over and we can check it out together?" he said, motioning for her with the magazine. "That is, unless you want your own space."

As much as she did appreciate the extra armrest,

she grabbed her Moscow mule and stepped across the aisle. As she settled in, she noticed that there was a subtle warmth that radiated from him, almost like she was sitting next to a space heater.

She had forgotten how he had always seemed to be just a few degrees hotter than her. At night, in the winter, she had loved getting into bed and setting her feet on his leg so she could get warm. He had complained about her icy toes, but at the same time he always moved closer to her when he knew she was chilly.

After she had lost their baby, all the things that had made her love him had vanished. It was as if all the little moments were erased the moment the nurse put the lifeless newborn into her arms.

She wasn't sure which one of them was no longer moving closer in bed at night after it had happened, but the days after their loss had broken them. Irreparably.

Or, at least she had thought.

She moved her foot closer to his, like she used to do when they were in bed with one another. Without seeming to realize, he bridged the distance between their feet until they were touching.

He leaned in, his shoulder brushing hers as he spoke about whatever article was on the page. It was something about a guest ranch in Wyoming, but she barely heard him. Rather, all she could think about was how his body felt against hers.

Be still her heart.

Though she should have moved away, and kept her distance from him, she found herself pulling in his scent—a mixture of his Aqua di Gio and fresh leather. She could feel her cheeks flushing as desire coursed through her.

Damn…

When they had been apart and a man had walked by wearing Eli's cologne, she had always taken notice, but none of them had ever smelled this good. Pheromones were for real.

She crossed her legs as she tried to gain control over her body. She wasn't a cavewoman who needed to cede her better judgment to her baser instincts. She was a grown-ass woman.

"Zoey?" he said like he had asked her a question and she had failed to respond.

"Yes," she said, trying to cover her lack of attention.

"You have been to a gentleman's club?" he asked, with a dumbfounded look that made it clear she had made a major error in not listening.

Crap.

"No…" she said, heat rising in her cheeks. "I mean, yes…but, no."

He folded the magazine and looked over at her. "Now I'm going to need to hear *that* story."

"Yeah, right. I already feel stupid enough without opening myself up for further scrutiny from you." She stuck out her tongue playfully.

"Oh, come on now. Did you dance on the pole?"

"Kiss my butt."

He laughed. "Just when it's getting good, you have to bring out something that much better."

The heat in her cheeks intensified. She hadn't meant it like *that*.

"You know very well that wasn't what I meant," she retorted.

He put his hands up in surrender and made an innocent face like he had no idea what she could have been referring to. "My apologies."

This was too close to flirting. Yeah, she loved the banter between them, but she had to nip it in the bud before it became more.

She caught another whiff of his cologne and he moved to put the magazine down on his table. She forced herself to check her grumble, a sound she was sure would be a mixture of desire and annoyance.

From the side of his chair, he pulled out his computer and handed it to her. "I was thinking that it would be good if you ran a scan, see if we can pick up your brother anywhere else in Sitges." There was a tightness in the way he spoke, as though he were uncomfortable with them growing emotionally closer, just as she was.

She was grateful for the change of direction. Neither of them needed to complicate their lives more than necessary.

Once this was over, and they had tracked down whoever put out the hit, she and Eli would both have to go back to their lives—lives that didn't revolve around one another.

No doubt, Eli would have to go back to Watch Dogs and begin work on another contract.

Though, maybe she could talk to her brothers about bringing him back on in STEALTH. Since she had started working mostly for their new military-grade tactical gear line, she had left a void in their company. He wasn't up to her level of tech acumen, but he could act as another hand. They needed someone they could trust.

She started running through the databases, pulling facial recognition and looking for her brother's features. There were a few vague hits, but nothing for the area and the time he would have been in Spain. Aside from his brief moment in the bank, it was as though he had disappeared.

The thoughts of all that could have happened to him crept into her consciousness, but she tried to sweep them away. It did her no good to think about whether Chad was alive or dead. As far as she was concerned, until she was one hundred percent certain of anything else, he was alive.

She grumbled.

"Finding anything?" he asked, careful to not look over her shoulder.

She had always appreciated a man who gave her space, especially when it came to her job.

"No, and it's starting to piss me off." She closed the computer and rubbed her hands over her face.

"Just because he isn't appearing anywhere right now doesn't mean we won't find signs of him tomorrow. You'll see," he said, but even she could hear the false optimism in his voice.

"You don't need to try and make me feel better—we both know that this may not turn out well. By now he may even be on the other side of the world. There's nothing to guarantee we're heading in the right direction." The thought made her stomach cramp.

"Your brothers are smart. Chad came out of hiding to appear at a bank—a place he knew he'd be on camera. He has to have known you were monitoring every eye in the sky for him. He did it on purpose."

Man, she hoped so.

"If that was the case, why didn't he give us more of an idea of what he is up to? Or where we can find him? Better yet, why not give us a sign to at least let us know he's okay?" She took a breath. "He would have sent me something to let me know he was safe—and yet…"

"Maybe he did. We could take another look at the video." He went to open the computer, but stopped as he glanced over at her.

"I have looked at that damned video at least a hundred times now. I've run every kind of test on the damn thing, and there's nothing. Nothing beyond what we already found."

"Did you pull the video of them leaving the bank?" Eli asked gently, trying not to get her even more riled up. "Maybe we could at least see which direction they headed?"

"There's nothing." She could feel the storm clouds

of a migraine rolling in. Eli was trying to help, and bless him for it, but he was crazy if he thought she hadn't exhausted every resource at her disposal to get a pinpoint on Chad's location.

She'd even looked deep into the dark web in hopes she could ID the woman at Chad's side, but it had been to no avail. The woman had been careful to not show too much of her face.

Though she loved and trusted her brothers to keep her safe and to do their best, there were only a few things in her life that she had ever trusted with every part of her soul. One was Trish, who was now gone, leaving her with her only other source of comfort— technology. It never let her down. It kept her safely tucked away from war zones but close enough that she could deal a deathblow upon faceless enemies. She could control the digital world like it was a ball of clay, only limited by her abilities—abilities that could give the world's best hackers a run for their money.

For the first time ever, she felt let down by the one thing she identified herself by. For there to be no more signs of Chad felt like there was a void in her heart, as well. But was it her abilities which failed her, or was it the machines she loved so much?

She was so very tired.

Like he could read her mind, Eli took the computer and put it away. "Let's just call it a night. When we get to Sitges, if your brother isn't there, so be it. We can call this expedition a vacation to the Med or something."

She sent him a drawn smile. "It's been a long time since I put my feet in the sand."

He cringed slightly as she spoke of sand, making her wish she had said something else instead.

"I just mean—" she started, hoping to correct her misstep.

"Do you remember that night in Tikrit?" Eli said, interrupting her.

"The night we were going to take down the leader in ISIL." She nodded as her thoughts moved to the cool night spent under the stars of the Iraqi desert. She had loved lying there, next to him, watching the darkened windows of the house for any sign of life in hopes that she and Eli could relay coordinates for the drone strike.

"Boots on the ground, baby," he said, quoting their old inside joke.

Whenever they were in a new place, a place they found they often hated either for the job or the people they were sent in to destroy, he'd always say, "Boots on the ground are worth a thousand in the office." And he'd always been right. It was part of the reason they were so highly sought after as a company. They always brought down their target.

It was his boots that were always on the ground, and the simple reminder was just his way of telling her he would catch her if she fell.

Eli glanced over his shoulder toward the rear of the plane. "There's a couch back there. I bet it folds out into a bed. Why don't you take this chance to relax? I have a feeling that when we get to Spain, the last thing on our minds is going to be sleeping.

There was a certain sadness that seeped into her as she looked over at Eli's strong green eyes, his wide-set jaw. Her gaze moved down to the muscles of his neck and the place where they gracefully melded into the burgeoning muscles of his chest. His pecs had gotten bigger since the two of them had gone their separate ways.

She gave herself a quick apprising glance. Maybe she should have put in a few more miles at the gym, but how could she have known she'd be hoping to attract a man—and not just any man, but Eli Wayne.

No, she was not trying to attract him. She couldn't be. They were friends. Only friends.

Just like before, with him so close to her, she wasn't sure that relaxation could possibly be in her future. But she was tired. And he was right; once they arrived it would be go-time.

"You don't think someone is running a decoy to flush us out of hiding, do you?" she asked. "I mean, think about it, even if the Gray Wolves have nothing to do with the hit out on Chad, they have to know of its existence. If so, they probably know we are looking for him. And what better way to have us come running than for us to spot him and fear for his safety?"

"How well do you know your enemies?"

She pursed her lips. "Well enough to know they would do anything it took to wipe us off the map."

There was a long silence between them, as he, too, must have realized the validity of her concerns. They may well have been walking into a trap—and it was quite possible that she and Eli wouldn't make it out of this one alive. One of the good things about her sending her brothers away was the fact they were unlikely to fall victim to the same fate.

At a certain level, she should have been afraid, but an odd sense of excitement filled her. It was like the threat of pending death made something click inside of her. Perhaps it was residual anger from the attacks at the ranch, or that someone was willing to use her brother to get to her, or maybe it was something else entirely, but she couldn't help feeling justified in making whoever was behind this pay.

"What are you thinking?" Eli asked.

"I'm thinking, if that's the case, and someone is setting up a trap for us, we should set it on its ear. Let's turn the hunters into the hunted."

He nodded, and his eyes brightened.

They weren't prey.

"If Chad really is behind us spotting him at the bank, then we have nothing to worry about, but if I'm right about others possibly being involved, we need to make a plan." She got up and walked back to the couch where, in front of it, was a small table with a pad of paper and a few magazines spread across the surface.

Eli followed her.

As they sat down, the flight attendant came out, refreshed their drinks and brought them each a sandwich before retiring to the front of the plane, closing the door behind her. Zoey couldn't remember the last time she'd eaten more than a few breath mints. Looking at the plate, her mouth watered. As Zoey took a bite of the pastrami sandwich, the mustard oozed out and a blob landed on the notepad on the table.

Eli laughed and she gave him the side-eye. As she did, he took a bite of his sandwich and a bit of mustard dribbled down the front of his shirt. "You know what I call that," she said with a chuckle, "*karma*. It serves you right for laughing at me." She nudged his knee as she teased him.

"For the record, I wasn't laughing at you." He dabbed at his button-up shirt with a napkin as they finished their sandwiches. "Actually, I was thinking about that little bistro where you and I went to dinner once. You know, the one where the guy played the accordion?"

She hadn't thought of that night in forever. That was when she had first told him she was expecting their child.

The little restaurant had been at the center of Avignon, an area seldom visited by tourists in one of the best eateries in the city. It was private and quiet. Their table had been just outside, set on the edge of the cobblestone street. When they had arrived, no one else was there as it was early and Eli had teased her for wanting to go to supper with blue hairs.

It had been a warm spring night, and the air was filled with the scent of lavender and the salty freshness of the sea. In many ways, the place was like the setting of a beloved rom-com in its perfection.

Was Eli bringing this up in order to talk about what had happened with their child, or was there another reason? She didn't want to ask him as she wasn't sure either of them was truly ready to confront the past.

"What about it?" she asked, hoping he would play by the unspoken rules that kept them from reopening those old wounds.

His eyes softened as he glanced at her, as he, too, must have been thinking of the news she had shared with him that night. "I think of that evening all the time. I often think about how beautiful you looked. Your hair was dyed black then—you remember?"

"I haven't dyed it black since then."

"You always look beautiful, no matter the color of your hair. But that night, there was just the right amount of sunshine to light up the strands of your raven hair. And when you turned, your hair would shimmer and take on faint hues of copper. I didn't tell you then, but you reminded me of a butterfly."

She took in a long breath. It had been so long ago, but he seemed to remember that night with crystalline clarity. In a way, she felt guilty for not remembering it nearly as well as he did, but her guilt was quickly replaced by endearment. He had definitely loved her once.

"A butterfly?" It seemed unreal that she could ever remind someone of something so delicate.

He nodded. "You were, and have always been, breathtaking."

For the second time that night, she could feel herself melting. No one spoke to her as he did. She had forgotten how charming and special he was—and how he could make her feel.

She wished she could be as eloquent and respond in a way that would make him feel as beloved, but she could come up with nothing. There were no words that would capture the tumultuous storm that filled her when he was near.

"Do you remember the song the guy was playing on the accordion?" he continued, graciously taking the pressure off her and only further reminding her of how wonderful he was.

She shook her head. That night had been mostly a blur thanks to the nerves and anxiety that she had felt knowing that she had to tell him that their lives were about to change.

"It was 'Falling in Love Again.'" He took her hand in his and she moved into him, putting her head on his shoulder as he lay back on the couch.

With a line like that, she couldn't have resisted the temptation to lie in his arms even if she had wanted to. For these few hours, she could let go and pretend the world wasn't waiting for them, that there was no hurt in the past, and this pocket of time was theirs forever.

As she listened to his heartbeat and the steady rhythm of his breathing, she thought of love. It was a strange word, a beautiful word, but odd nonetheless. It was a single syllable, and a word that could be said in a simple breath. It could mean a thousand different things: an emphasis added flippantly to everything from pizza to lovers, or it could be a whispered promise of forever, or it could be shouted to the heavens as a way to say goodbye. To every person, every relationship, every moment, it meant something different.

Their love, that love of the past, was gone. They had carried its weight together for years. Sometimes it had been like a feather, while at others it had been like a bag of stones—one that threatened to drown them in the depths of life.

Once she had let it go, *that* love was gone, forever.

She liked to think they could find a new definition for the feelings that welled within her as he ran his fingers down the length of her arm, making goose bumps rise on her skin.

But she wasn't sure if she was ready, as love could also be defined as fear.

Chapter Twelve

He had made so many mistakes in his life, but none had been greater than watching Zoey leave him and doing nothing about it. They had both been hurting, and yet instead of moving closer to her, he had felt himself growing further away. At the time, he thought it would protect him, but he had also thought it would protect her. He had so much anger in those days.

That anger had quickly turned to rage and destruction—but the one thing he hadn't wanted to bring down and destroy was what they had built together.

Once he had heard a statistic that couples that experienced a stillbirth were twenty-two percent more likely than the average couple to break up.

They had never really talked about having children, but when he learned he was to be a father the world shifted beneath him. Colors were brighter. Food tasted better. It was easier to get through the day. His anxiety lessened. Everything, even down to the way he brushed his teeth, changed. With the knowledge that they were having a baby came the feeling that his life now truly held purpose. It was strange, but he found comfort in the idea that he had been put on this planet to do something more. He was a father.

During those few blissful months, nothing else mattered—only them, their love and the family they were going to build.

And just like that, when he saw the pale, lifeless face of his daughter, it was all stripped away.

Though years had passed, there was still an ache in his heart as he recalled all they had lost.

Though there was no going back in time and there was no fixing the hurt that still lay between them, as he touched her skin, he allowed himself to pretend the well of pain had finally run dry.

He kissed the top of her head and she sighed, the sound relaxed and pleased. She must have felt as safe as he did. They had found one another again.

She moved against him, lifting his hand to her lips and kissing his fingers. Her touch was so unexpectedly sensual that his body stirred to life. He ran his thumb over the soft pink curves of her lips and as he did, she smiled and looked up at him.

He knew that look. Oh, that saucy, sexy look. Any resistance his body had in awakening fell away.

He wanted her. And there was no doubt in his mind that she wanted him.

They could surrender to this moment and let it

erase the last bits of their feelings from the past. But there would be no going back if they went down this wonderful, erotic path.

Zoey had always been an animal in bed. Hands down the best he'd ever had.

When she made love, her body was like rose petals opening and curling as they came into the rays of ecstasy.

In watching her body move, he had always been forced to be mindful as he feared letting himself go and cutting short the beauty before him.

If he could spend a million lifetimes watching her atop of him, it would still not have been long enough.

There was nothing, and no one who could compare to her.

Part of what made her who she was were also a few broken pieces. Some of those pieces were from family, friends and former lovers, but too many of the cracks were put there by him. If he wanted a future with her, he needed to work to help her heal those parts or he would risk losing her again.

The thought of never having her in his arms had haunted him for too long as it was. He couldn't go back to living that way. If that meant not having sex with her, or limiting how far they went right now, it was a sacrifice he was willing to make.

He needed her. Forever.

And though they were close right now, one misstep, and Zoey would pull away. It was what she did. It had taken him so long to break down those walls the last time, and he had been foolish enough to allow them to be rebuilt in his absence.

He would need to be careful doing what he knew needed to be done. He didn't want her to feel rejected. That was the last thing that he could allow to happen. She could be so strong, so resilient, but if he chipped at her ego there was no question that she would resent him for it.

She moved her body up his, rubbing her hand over his pants in her ascent. "Did you ever think of me when we were apart?" she cooed.

"Every minute of every day."

She paused for a moment, reading his face like she wasn't sure whether or not she could believe him.

Didn't she know he wasn't like other dudes? He didn't need one-liners to get a woman in bed.

"Did you think of this?" she whispered, her breath brushing against his lips even more gently than his finger had brushed over hers.

She leaned in, and their lips met. Bursts of endorphins exploded in his brain, making him feel as though little fireworks were going off throughout his body. Though it felt amazing, he was certain that if he allowed them to continue, he would undoubtedly get burned.

But he couldn't pull away.

Not yet.

He reached up, spreading his fingers through her loose hair as he cupped her face in his hands.

She tasted of vodka, ginger, the past and a hint of

the future. He had almost forgotten what it felt like to kiss her, the way she sucked in a breath and released it as a low, throaty moan as her body moved against him.

Climbing atop him, she straddled him and rocked her hips.

Damn.

He wanted to rip off her clothes and take her there. Forget the consequences. Just feel her. All of her.

She rolled again, and her breasts rubbed against his cheek as she moved.

He couldn't stop his tender, lusty hum as he buried his face in her cleavage. She smelled of sweet sweat and the fragrance he knew so well.

It was all too much. If he didn't turn away now, he would never be able to.

If he took the risk and made love to her, so many things could go wrong.

He kissed the supple skin of her left breast, then the right in greeting. It had been so long and after tonight, he might never have the chance to be this close to her heart again.

His lips grazed her cashmere skin as he pulled back and lowered his head against her chest.

He wanted it all. Everything they had to offer. And, in the stolen moment, he knew that was more than either of them could give.

"You are fantastic." He exhaled, trying to gain control over his body and his mind.

"I can't believe we are here again. I've missed

you." She ran her fingers through his hair, gently tugging as she moved.

"I've missed you, too," he said, hoping she would not misread what he needed to say. "Every day I thought of you and our child."

She leaned back from him, like the word *child* was an electric shock to her system. That wasn't the reaction he had wanted, but he wasn't surprised. There would always be pain there no matter how much time went by.

But they needed to move forward. Even if it wasn't together, a pain like that must be confronted, dealt with and then not allowed to embitter. If allowed, pain like that could break a person. He knew all too well, as it had broken him.

He would never forget the promises that had grown in her belly, and the dreams of a future that never came, but he couldn't keep reliving their loss. That was no kind of life.

She said nothing as she looked at him. In a way, he was glad she did not want to talk about the baby, especially now. And perhaps he had made a mistake in bringing it up, but it had fallen from his lips thanks to the purple haze created in his mind by her touch.

"I want you," he said, his hands drifting down until they rested on her fleshy hips. She was so close to perfect, that it pained him to see her looking at him like that, like she was just waiting for the next zap.

Which made what he had to say that much harder.

The old adage of *damned if you do, damned if you don't* popped into his head.

"You know I want you," he said, moving beneath her so she could feel exactly what she did to him. "But I'm... I think if we do this, you'll come to resent me."

She opened her mouth as if to speak, but slowly closed it again. It was as if she wanted to argue with him, to tell him what he was saying wasn't true, but she must have realized he was right.

"We only just came back into each other's lives, and I don't know that either one of us is healed enough. I'm afraid if we do this, and you let me back in your life like this, I'm going to want to stay in it. And I can't lose you. I can't go through that kind of heartache ever again. You tore out my heart."

There was a slight sheen to her eyes, and she blinked back the start of her tears. "I get it, Eli. I wish none of that had ever happened," she whispered.

He wanted to tell her that she had done nothing wrong, that he could understand her reaction and why she had screamed out of his life. However, he didn't completely understand. And even if she tried to explain it to him, he wasn't sure that would ever make it okay. But what he did understand was that there was no going back in time. There were no redos.

There was only forgiveness.

"Thank you. And I'm sorry for pulling away. I just didn't know how to deal with everything."

"I didn't, either." She moved off him, saving him the agony of having to tell her that he couldn't make love to her right now. "I often wonder if our jobs destroy a certain element of our soul that makes us capable of being vulnerable. You know?" She moved to the couch beside him and picked up her drink, taking a long sip like it was a salve for the wounds that rested within her.

He wasn't sure he agreed. He felt pretty damned vulnerable right now.

She set her glass down, ice clinking against the sides of the cup like a bell tolling to mark a funeral. Sadness welled within him. Though logically he had known the decision to pull away was right, it felt as though he was losing her again as he watched her stand up and walked back to her seat.

Her movements carried an air of finality— an air he had seen before.

HE TRIED TO catch some sleep on the rest of the flight, but what little he had gotten was spent restless with dreams of firefights and lost battles. Every time he looked over at Zoey, she was clicking away on her computer and carefully ignoring him.

The ground they had gained in their friendship seemed lost.

Maybe it was better this way. Some hurts were just too big, too defining, too much.

As the wheels of the jet touched down, she finally looked up at him. Her eyes were bloodshot, and he would have assumed she had been crying if he hadn't known better—she had never been the kind to shed a tear, not when she could stuff away emotions and try to forget they were there.

"We will find him," Eli said, decidedly turning the conversation away from them and back to just her. She and her family needed the most help right now. The rest could wait.

"I hope so. I looked everywhere, but found nothing." There was a depth in her voice that made him unsure exactly what she meant.

He wanted to tell her that life had a way of working things out as they should be, but even he didn't believe that. Life was a constant kick in the butt.

"We'll keep looking. We won't stop looking until we find him, I promise."

She smiled as she stood up and motioned for him to take the lead. As they made their way out of the plane, the Spanish heat washed over them. The city smelled of dust, poverty and the forgotten sea.

The airport staff loaded their luggage into the waiting car as they got in. It didn't take long to get on the highway that led to Sitges and their waiting hotel.

As they drove, they passed by the wall of catacombs, the few occupants of the city who seemed interested in the ocean that washed against the city's stony cliffs. The graves were walled in glass and as they passed by, curiosity drove him to search for the skeletons of the long dead.

The city of the dead was macabre and strangely

beautiful, a far cry from the American style of death and memorial in which loved ones were forgotten and tucked away at the edges of society. Here, they were given a view, a place in everyday life, and thought of even by those, like him, who bore no ancestry.

As they twisted through the tunnels carved into the mountainsides, he thought about his searching of the graves. Perhaps there was something really wrong with him in the fact that instead of focusing on what could be, he found himself searching for ashes and bone.

When they arrived at the small European-style hotel, they were ushered in by staff and called by name. Zoey made a point of grabbing her bag, as though she were afraid someone might steal it.

As they checked in and followed the bellhop toward their room, she leaned into him and whispered, "Do you think everybody in Spain knows we're here?"

He chuckled, but beneath his mirth was the realization she may have been right. People were watching them as they strode through the lobby. "There's plenty of tourists that come to this area. We're going to blend right in."

She glanced around as they made their way up the set of double-winding staircases. The place was quiet, the only sounds besides their footsteps and the slight humming coming from the bellhop was the chatter from a small bar offset from the lobby.

He had made sure to get two rooms that adjoined

one another thanks to a small interior door. He would leave it up to her whether or not she left the door unlocked. Either way, he wasn't sure he minded—by giving her the decision, it kept his mind from running in circles.

He watched her enter her room. With a nod, she closed the door behind her.

He had been wrong in thinking they could take their relationship to the next level in the future. Though the world would always keep moving forward, and they could function as a team, they had proven that two people could go through the motions of the present and stay firmly entrenched in the past.

Chapter Thirteen

Zoey couldn't believe she had let things get that far with Eli yesterday. As fun as it was to fantasize about being with him again, reality was another thing entirely. There was a chasm of wounds between them that ran too deep and too wide for them to ever cross.

It was never her intention to hurt him, rather just save herself. She had known that there would be collateral damage when she left, but she had thought he was so much stronger than the man who had kissed her last night.

She looked at the door that rested between the two hotel rooms. For a second, she thought about going over there and opening the door and letting him back into her life. But she wasn't sure she was ready. Instead, she scrolled through her phone and looked for more search results in hopes of finding Chad. Nothing. Always nothing.

A few times throughout the night, she had wondered if the video they had seen at the bank was even real. It was almost as if he were a ghost, slipping in and out of this world and teasing her with his presence.

She pulled a hair dye kit out of her bag and went to the bathroom. The pink had started to fade in her hair, and though she knew she could fit in with any color hair here in Spain, she decided on brown teak. The color was bland and indistinguishable from the masses. Hopefully, she could dress down enough to disappear. The last thing she needed was for them to be spotted before they could get in touch with Chad.

There was a knock on the front door as she let the color set.

She took one look at herself in the mirror. There was nothing sexier than a woman wearing a clear plastic shower cap and yesterday's makeup. Maybe this was what Eli needed to see in order to bring him back into the reality of who she really was.

But as she walked to the door, she hurriedly tried to wipe the mascara from under her eyes.

There was another knock at the door, more impatient this time.

"I'm coming." She opened the door, and standing there in the hallway was room service complete with silver platters of Spanish pastries and silver-domed plates on a fully loaded rolling trolley.

"I have the breakfast your friend ordered," the man pushing the trolley said as he struggled to look anywhere but at the mess on her head.

She stepped back and motioned for him to bring the trolley into the room. As the man walked by her, the scent of oatmeal, coffee, sausage, beans and eggs wafted toward her and made her mouth water. She reached into her wallet and grabbed some cash for the man as he made his way out.

Eli must have known she would forget to order breakfast for herself. As she closed the door, she caught another glimpse of herself in the mirror. Perhaps she was getting to see who Eli really was, as well.

Washing the dye from her hair and face, she wrapped a towel around her head. The dye had done its job, and she couldn't help but notice she looked like her mother.

She went to the door between their rooms and knocked gently. She wasn't going to eat his breakfast alone. Not when he had been so thoughtful. It didn't escape her attention that he may well have done it on purpose to force her hand and invite him to her room. Either way, whether it was selfless or selfish, she couldn't deny the fact that she was glad to have him with her. Though he had implied that there was no room for a relationship between them, perhaps they could go on to be friends when this was all through.

She smiled at the thought just as the door opened. Eli was dressed for the day in a linen shirt, perfectly suited for the heat, and a pair of khaki utility shorts. There was a slight bulge at his waist. He was strapped.

The realization that he was carrying a gun came as a comfort.

He looked her over, his gaze settling on the towel still wrapped around her head. "Are we going for a more devil-may-care look today? Do I need to go back and change my clothes?" he teased, jabbing a thumb in the direction of his room.

"Actually—" she walked over to her bag and grabbed the bulletproof shirt she had brought along just for him "—put this on." She tossed him the pale blue button-up.

He caught it midair. "Crap, was I supposed to bring you an outfit, too? Or is this a new uniform style for STEALTH?"

He slipped off his linen shirt, throwing it onto his bed. She tried not to look at his faintly lined abs and thick-muscled arms before he pulled on the new shirt.

"Just consider yourself lucky," she said. "Now, shut up and get in here and eat breakfast."

He laughed as he stepped into her room and closed his door behind him. He walked over to the tray of food and started lifting off some of the domes and lids. There was a medley of foods from fruit and meats, to grains and cheeses. "I know you're normally just a coffee girl in the morning, but I wanted to make sure you ate well. I don't know when we'll get a chance to grab some lunch."

She stepped over to the trays and poured each of them a cup of coffee.

He grabbed a plate and started stacking food on it, and she followed suit. After the long flight and all the time changes, her body was begging for food.

As she lifted the last lid to peek inside, she dropped the silver dome with a clatter. Eli stopped. He picked up the lid exposing what lay underneath. Upon a plate, garnished with parsley and decorative orange slices, was the tip of a man's trigger finger. Next to it on the plate was a simple note that read Welcome to Spain.

"Son of a—" Zoey said under her breath.

Their arrival hadn't gone unnoticed. Someone was tracking them.

"I can't wait to see what they put in my eggs," Eli said, laughing as he set the lid on the cart next to the plate.

"Wow, so glad you haven't matured at all since the last time we were together," she said, but couldn't help the little giggle that escaped her. Truth be told, she had always loved the fact that he could take the darkest moments of their jobs and relieve the stress by making a joke of it. "Who do you think the finger belongs to?"

Eli shrugged. "I have no idea."

She took a picture and sent it to Mindy and Sabrina with a text asking them to pull anything they could from it. "You don't think it's Chad's, do you?"

His face pinched, making it clear he thought that it was her brother's.

No.

She forgot about the food as she threw on a pair of cutoff jeans and her Nirvana tank top. She slipped her phone into the back of her shorts pocket, covering it with her T-shirt. "Let's go."

He didn't argue, thankfully. They had no real starting point, no direction and no idea what the future would bring, but they couldn't sit in their hotel room and just fester. If she had to go house by house and knock on every door in the entire country of Spain to get Chad back and to ensure he was safe, she would do it.

As she moved to the door of her room, Eli stopped her. "There's still a towel on your head."

She huffed. Of course there was. She pulled it off and rubbed the last bit of wetness from her hair and threw the towel to the floor. Not bothering to look at herself in the mirror, she grabbed her bags and checked out of the hotel and headed out the door, Eli close on her heels.

Pulling up an encrypted map, she led the way toward the bank. The streets were narrow, just wide enough in most places to accommodate a single car or gaggle of tourists. She looked up at the historic buildings around her, hoping to see cameras installed sporadically, but she found none. No wonder she had a hard time finding images of Chad. Perhaps he was still here.

The bank was located near the main thoroughfare in the small town. From the street in front, she could see the Mediterranean. At the beach, children were laughing as they played and splashed in the water.

What it would have been like to have another life.

She walked to the front door of the bank, and tried to open the door, but it was locked. It wasn't until now that she realized how early it was. They wouldn't be open for another fifteen minutes.

Though it was stupid, she couldn't help feeling like she had failed. She always thought she was so smart, so strong, and yet here they stood in the middle of a foreign city with nothing but days-old information. She had to do better.

She hated to think of what Eli thought of her ineptitude. He had come all this way to help her, and there she was, unable to help herself.

It was a good thing she wasn't a crier.

"It's going to be okay," he said as he stepped close, running his fingers through her hair and taking a moment to fix what she assumed was her best attempt at a rat's nest.

Though she knew the sweet action was meant to soothe, she was so annoyed with herself that she stepped back and out of his touch. As she moved, she noticed the bulge under Eli's shirt and a thought crossed her mind.

"Are you all right?" Eli asked, seeming surprised by her edginess.

Opening up her phone. She looked up at him and smiled. "Yeah, I just had an idea." She clicked on the video of her brother and zoomed in on the woman in the background and skipped ahead to the moment the girl turned from the frame. At the woman's waist was a small bulge. As Zoey moved the video clip by clip, a small black handgun briefly came into view.

She zoomed down even further.

She knew that gun, or at least she was almost certain she did.

It looked like the ones used in the phony arms deals with the Gray Wolves. They had been promised as part of the shipments that they had used to lure the Gray Wolves into the trap they were planning before everything went haywire and Trish was killed.

Which meant…

She clapped her hand over her mouth with excitement as she hopped from one foot to the other. Though she probably looked like a madwoman dancing around in the city streets, she didn't care. Finally, they had a break.

She turned the phone for Eli to see and pointed at the gun. As she did, she glanced up and stopped as she realized that, just like with Chad, this bank was rolling footage. Thankfully, her phone's screen was turned away from the cameras. Her face on the other hand…

"We have to go." She nodded in the direction of the cameras and Eli's gaze instinctively moved toward them.

Without another word, they made their way from the bank, going in the opposite direction from which they came in the event anyone was watching. Not that it probably mattered—someone already knew they were there and was likely just waiting for the perfect moment to strike them down.

They made their way several blocks from the bank before slowing down. She kept checking over her shoulder, making sure they weren't being followed, but everyone around them seemed caught up in their own comings and goings and not focused on them.

The finger in the room was just a threat. If whoever had sent it had wanted her dead, she would've been dead by now. Obviously, they had access to her room, so it had to be some type of message.

"Now what were you going to tell me?" Eli asked.

"The gun in the video, it has a tracker in it. When we were doing the gun deal with the Gray Wolves, we had all the guns we were going to sell them implanted with GPS devices." Pulling out her phone, she clicked to the locator.

"How do you know it's one of your guns?" Eli asked.

"I don't for certain, but it's the best damn thing I can think of right now." Her stomach flopped like an undercooked pancake.

Going back to the enhanced video, she tried to read the serial number stamped into the barrel, but she could only pull the first four digits. Hopefully, it would be enough.

They walked around aimlessly as she tapped away on her phone, moving down the list of possible serial numbers of the guns they had planted with the trackers. After a few minutes, she came up with a list of twenty-five possible guns.

They stopped in front of the Iglesia de San Bartolome y Santa Tecla Catholic church, and with an acknowledging look, they ducked inside. In the church, they would be safe from prying eyes.

Their footsteps echoed on the stone floors, reverberating against the walls and echoing back at them thanks to the large domed ceiling and empty expanses. The cathedral was awe-inspiring with its breathtaking gold-inlaid ceiling, grand organ and pristine marble-white walls. It was different from the other churches she had seen in her years spent around Europe in its fine craftsmanship but simple design.

Genuflecting, they made their way to a pew in the back of the church and sat down. The pews creaked as they moved, making the room seem even emptier than it was.

"Take half the list, see if you can pinpoint the trackers to anywhere within three hundred miles." She mirrored her phone to his.

"What if we are just chasing our tails?" he asked.

She bit back the urge to be annoyed. "Do you have a better idea?"

He looked like she had struck him, and she instantly regretted saying anything. But seriously, why would he speak out? She was doing the best she could. And damn him if it wasn't good enough.

He tapped on his phone. "I'm going to send the protective ops STEALTH team into our hotel. Maybe they can get the finger and see if they can pull some DNA or something. At least that way, we can know that it isn't Chad's."

That test would take weeks, they both knew it,

but she appreciated his efforts. "Hopefully we have Chad back long before the results."

He nodded and the defeat in his eyes grew like a storm cloud just waiting to break loose. "Are you upset with me?" he asked.

She sighed as she put her phone down in her lap. She hadn't been after a fight, not in the slightest, but he seemed to be gearing himself up for one. Though she didn't have the wherewithal to deal with it, she had little choice. If they were going to continue working together, they were going to have to talk about the elephant in the room. "I'm not upset."

"Then what is going on with you? Did I do something wrong? If so, seriously, I apologize." He leaned closer to her and took her hand in his.

She wasn't sure what to do with it, but she liked the fact that in one moment he could be pulling the trigger and killing the enemy, and holding her hand as if it were a Fabergé egg in the next. He was the best of both worlds—lethal and protective.

It seemed impossible, but in the years that had passed, he had become even more like her dream man.

"You're good. I'm just…" *protecting my heart… terrified of falling in love…worried about my brother…scared of losing even more…* She could think of a hundred ways to end her sentence, but none of her many thoughts pressed past her lips. Being so open with him would not serve any purpose. "I'm just trying to focus on Chad." She squeezed his fingers, then let go of his hand.

No matter how great Eli was or how badly she wanted to live in the fuzzy, warm safe haven provided by his kiss, there wasn't room in her heart for anything right now—not with her brother and her family in mortal danger. For now, her only focus could be on survival.

Chapter Fourteen

Though he'd thought he had made the right choice by not having sex with her on the plane, now he wasn't so sure. She had taken it as a rejection, just as he had feared she would. There was no going back for another chance— especially sitting in the middle of the church. It had felt taboo even taking her hand in the sacred place.

He took one more look at her hand as he tapped on his phone, trying to find the location of the weapon the woman with Chad had been carrying.

He had been stupid for saying anything to Zoey about her idea. She was frazzled. He'd seen the desperation in her eyes the moment he opened the door between their rooms this morning and when they had found the finger... Well, that had definitely pushed her over the edge.

In all likelihood, and as much as he didn't want to admit it to Zoey, the finger belonged to Chad. Why else would anyone leave such a macabre threat for them to find?

The only time he'd ever seen anything like that, aside from mob movies, was when a member of his team had found a bloody foot stuffed in their duffel bag. Two weeks later the guy had been killed in action by a stray bullet. Everyone on his assigned team had their suspicions about why the bullet had found him, specifically that someone within their crew had a bone to pick. But he had always doubted the likelihood of something like that happening. His teams were always the best of the best—friendly fire wasn't in their vocabulary.

He moved to the tenth serial number on his list of guns. Tapping the number into the search, a green dot appeared on his map. There, in the center of Sitges, just blocks from where they sat, he had found a possible location. "Holy—" He stopped before the rest of the words fell from his mouth and landed like a thud in the center of the pew.

"Huh?" she asked, looking up from her screen.

"You were right," he whispered, glancing around and ensuring that they were still alone.

He could have sworn a light shone down as he said those words to the woman sitting next to him.

"Um, what? Do you want to repeat that?" she said, raising one eyebrow. "Did you just say I was *right*?"

"Live it up," he said, teasing back. "Look." He lifted his phone for her to see the little green speck on his screen.

She jumped to her feet. "I knew it!" A smile spread across her face and finally some of the darkness faded from her features. "He's here. I knew he was here."

Just because they were close to that dot didn't mean they were any closer to reaching finding Chad or finding him *alive*.

But Eli had already been wrong once. Hopefully he would be wrong again.

She took his phone out of his hand and, without missing a beat, flew through the doors of the church and out onto the street in the direction of the dot.

He followed along, watching her hair glistening in the morning sun. The new color was beautiful on her and, as she moved, the sunlight picked up bits of burgundy like her hair was imbued with rubies.

She was nearly running as she made her way around a corner and toward the apartment building in the distance where the dot was centered. The building had clean, clear lines and was painted a vibrant yellow with black art deco accents. At each arched window sat wrought-iron balconies. It was a place where only the well-heeled could afford to reside— a far cry from the derelict back alley room where he would have expected Chad to have been held hostage.

He touched Zoey's arm, stopping her midstride. "Wait."

"What? He's waiting," she said, nudging her chin in the direction of the building just half a block down the avenue.

"We can't just run in there half-cocked. Who knows what, or who, will be in there."

Her face fell. "Do you think we should call Trevor and Jarrod, let them know what we've found? See if they want to fly over?"

He shrugged. More wasn't necessarily better in this situation. "Let's just keep an eye on this place, see who's coming and going. I would hate it if we walked into a trap."

She chewed on her lip and nodded. Taking one last look at the building, she walked down an alley to their right, and out of view of whoever could have been inside the building in question.

"Lucky for us, I have friends in the NSA who understand our need to glean information from their drones on occasion… Without asking permission… Or actually telling them…" She tapped on the screen, pulling up what he was absolutely certain were illegal images from her near and dear "friends" within USCYBERCOM.

He chuckled. That was the Zoey he knew, doing anything she needed to do to take care of business. The Watch Dogs had an IT crew, a faceless man he had never met, and their intel collection was good, but it was nothing like Zoey on a mission.

Once again, he found himself missing his old role as Zoey's attaché.

For a moment, he considered what it would be like if they could go back in time and revisit the mistakes of his past. If they hadn't risked their friendship by moving things to the next level, they would probably still have been working in the same group, united against one enemy. She would know, without a doubt, that he was someone she could turn to and trust. Instead he'd let his body take the lead, and it had led them straight into disaster.

"Getting anything?" he asked.

Looking at her screen, he could just make out the area where they stood from the eye in the sky, he could see her new brown locks and what he feared was a possible future bald spot on the crown of his head. He was surprised everything was so immediate, so real-time. Out of curiosity, he raised his hand and instantly he watched himself doing it on her phone. If they had had this tech five years ago—heck, even two years ago—many of their failed missions surely would've turned out differently.

"Damn, I had no idea our government had come this far." He gave a little whistle.

She looked up from the screen and nodded. "Doesn't your new team have access to any kind of technology, Jiminy Cricket?"

She said *new team* like it was the name of his new girlfriend.

"Why, Ms. Zoey Martin, are you jealous?" he asked with a smirk.

"Why would I be jealous of some two-bit operation that can't even hack their way into the most basic of the government's databases?"

If she thought that the NSA's drone encryption keys were basic, he couldn't help but wonder what the more complicated ones were hiding.

He resisted the urge to ask if she could rewind it, fearing that he would sound like he was a thousand years old and from a different planet.

"Here we go," she said, moving closer to him so they could watch the screen side by side. "This was from early this morning."

She clicked Play. There was the normal movement of people up and down the street in front of the apartment building where the GPS device was located—nothing stood out. She skipped ahead two minutes. A woman wearing a light gray peacoat stepped out of the front doors of the building. The woman was alone. Even though she was wearing large welding mask–sized sunglasses, it was easy to recognize her as the woman from the bank's video.

The woman stopped and reached for something in her tiny purse and then started walking toward where he and Zoey now stood. He looked up from the phone, half expecting the woman in the coat to be standing directly in front of him. Instead, there was the buzz of car horns in the distance and the shuffle of feet on the cobblestone as people walked past.

The woman pranced like a well-trained and expensive dog.

"Do you see the handbag she's carrying?" Zoey asked, zooming in on the brown bag. It had a silver chain as the strap and it looked strange on the tiny briefcase-looking purse.

"What about it? I mean, besides being stupid-looking." He never understood what women saw in purses. As far as he was concerned, a purse was a purse was a purse. It was just a place to put their crap until they needed their crap. Really, a paper sack would do in a pinch.

"First, it isn't *stupid* looking." She gave him a quick look up and down. "You are hardly one to judge, Mr. Cargo Shorts and a button-up."

"It's practical," he argued, but was stopped by the wave of her hand.

"More importantly," she continued, "the bag she is carrying is Jean Vitton. It's this year's Petite Malle mini bag."

"That doesn't change the fact that it looks like something from the bargain bin at the dollar store."

She huffed, clearly annoyed with his commentary on fashion. "Regardless of what you feel about this purse, it's amazing."

He cocked his head and gave her a disapproving look. "Really? You *like* the purse? It looks like a dude's shrunken briefcase. And I know for a fact that you are more comfortable carrying around a rucksack than you are an expensive purse."

"A rucksack is *practical*," she said, smirking as she threw his words back at him. "That being said, I am still a woman. While this one may not exactly be my style it doesn't change the fact that it is Vitton's most expensive purse this season and it isn't even available in stores yet."

"Oh, fancy."

"Actually, yeah, it is." She smiled like she knew

something he didn't. "With a bag like that, we can probably figure out who she is. They only give those bags out to the rich and famous."

"Sounds like you just want to make a stop at Jean Vitton."

"So what if I do? But I think I can get what we need without going there." She pulled up a new window on her phone and set to work, starting at the Jean Vitton website. From there, she broke into their mainframe, hacking her way straight into the sales records.

It wasn't the first time she'd terrified him. With a tiny bit of information this woman could do almost anything—and put nearly any federal agent to shame. If anything, she'd gotten even better at her job since the last time he'd seen her. It had to be so hard doing what she did, constantly being on the forefront of technology, a world that changed nearly every second. He would happily remain a point man for as long as he still had a job.

"So according to their sales records, they've only sold five of these purses so far. They've given three away. And there is a wait list." She looked up. "I bet if I put my address in here, they would send us one for free." Her fingers trembled over the screen like she was seriously contemplating using her skill set to rig the system for herself. "The first person on the wait list is Gigi Hadid. Think about it, I can have the same purse as Gigi."

"I have no idea who that even is." He reached

over and took the phone from her. "I still don't get it. I mean, how much is this purse worth anyways?"

"Twenty Gs." There was a breathless air to her words.

He handed the phone back to her like by simply touching the phone he was implicating himself in the theft of something so expensive. Now he *really* didn't get it. "You do know, for that kind of money you could get yourself a hell of a tactical setup."

She laughed. "I am more than a little aware of that." She gave him a look like he was the dumbest man on the planet.

"Oh, yeah. I bet you can get your tac gear on the cheap. But still, I would much rather have good gear than some stupid purse."

"Call it a stupid purse again and I am going to do the active-round testing of my next tactical line on you." There was fire in her eyes, but he knew she was teasing.

"Okay, so there's some things I don't understand. I'm sure I'll never get it." He put his hands up in surrender. "As for this fine specimen of fashion that is this purse, who are the five lucky souls chosen to possess such magnificence?"

She couldn't keep a straight face, no matter how badly she wanted to continue chastising him for his bad taste. "There are several socialites, one Hollywood star and one that interests me," she said.

"And that is?"

"According to this, there was one that was sold

to a foreign buyer. Looks like it was picked up in Dubai."

"What was the name of the foreign buyer?" he asked.

"It was bought by a woman named Shaye Griest."

That name meant nothing to him. "Okay?" he said.

"You ever heard of Kristen Griest or Shaye Haver?"

He shook his head.

"Kristin and Shaye were the only women ever to graduate from the army ranger school. These are two badass women."

"I don't understand what two rangers have to do with one purse." He racked his brain in trying to put it together.

"When I was poking around about the Algerian prime minister and his family, I found that his oldest daughter used to be active on social media. She tweeted about Kristin and Shaye and what it means to her that these two women were able to develop their skills in such a prestigious and competitive location."

He still didn't get it, and apparently the look on his face must've said as much.

"That's the pseudonym for the prime minister's daughter, *dude*." She shook her head in exasperation.

"Oh," he grumbled, trying to cover his embarrassment. Hopefully she'd never realized how much better a catch she was than him. If she did, he would never have a chance in getting her back.

"Do you think that Chad is shacking up with the Algerian prime minister's daughter?" Eli asked.

"Or she kidnapped him." Zoey shrugged.

"Something about all of this isn't making sense. Why would the Algerian government put a hit out on Chad if he was with the Algerian prime minister's daughter? Wouldn't it put her in danger?"

Zoey nodded. "I know. I was thinking the same thing."

"Are you sure the woman carrying the bag is the PM's daughter?"

"So far, in every video I've seen of her, this girl has been very careful to cover her face—it's like she knows people will be using facial recognition to look for her," Zoey said. She started pulling up videos and images of the woman on her phone.

The woman had long dark, almost black hair in the most recent official government photos posted by the Algerians. However, the woman standing outside the building with the big sunglasses was unquestionably blonde. As he stared at the images in front of him, he could make out the same subtle curves of her jaw. And her nose was blunt and slightly upturned like a short ski jump. He couldn't say with one hundred percent certainty that the woman from the drone's image and the Algerian prime minister's daughter were the same woman, but he couldn't deny it, either. It was certainly within the realm of possibility.

"Did you see anything on the video about Chad?" he asked.

She gave a resigned sigh. "Not yet, but that doesn't mean he's not holed up in there."

There was the clatter of the metal gate being pushed up as the bistro behind them opened up for lunch. The woman who must've worked there gave them a smile and said something in Spanish to which Zoey replied.

They needed to get out of there, before they were tracked down again. Zoey turned off her phone and stashed it in her pocket.

They couldn't go back to their hotel and they couldn't keep running. He wasn't sure what they should do next, but inaction was almost more dangerous than moving on their target. "Can you do facial recognition on the video from the drone for Chad?"

"Already done. Nothing came up, but he could have gone in the building during the night or when the drone wasn't posted at this location." There was a desperation to her voice.

Her unchecked emotions made Eli that much more on edge. It wasn't like Zoey to just say what she was feeling or even not bother to disguise it… She was hurting, which made pain rise within him. In a way, the situation reminded him of the last time they'd been together with their baby.

If he failed her, if Chad was hurt or killed, he would feel just as guilty as he had that day. Though he was certain he was doing the right thing, he hadn't taken all of the consequences into consideration. Here he was thinking about coming back to work with the Martins, but he was far more likely to find himself back on Zoey's persona non grata list than back in her life.

Maybe he would've been better off getting her flowers instead of chasing her halfway across the state in order to catch a glimpse of her. As he chuckled at the thought, he knew he was lying to himself. He would give up his last breath for her. No matter how this went down, there was no way he could stop loving her.

"What's the prime minister's daughter's real name?" he asked.

"Nihad Almaz," she said without a pause. "She is one of three daughters and a son. The son is involved with the Algerian military, and there is talk that he will one day run the country in his father's footsteps."

"Is there any talk about how his daughters feel about that?" Eli took her hand and they started slowly walking around the city, keeping the apartment building in view.

"They haven't said anything publicly about the situation, but it looks as though they are going to act as ambassadors for the country until the time of their marriages."

"None of them are married?" Eli thought of Chad. What if this wasn't a kidnapping, but rather an elopement? Though Zoey seemed to be convinced that this wasn't a romance. But if it *was*, it would explain why the prime minister would put out large sums of money for Chad's head.

But that didn't explain the severed finger that had been served to them this morning beside their toast and eggs. Or why the PM would put his own flesh and blood in the line of fire. That was, unless the man didn't care about his daughter's welfare. It wasn't unheard of for a father to disown a daughter, or son who moved against the family.

Chad had to know they were looking for him, and he wouldn't just run off with a woman and not give his family a heads-up. There were so many things that just weren't making sense.

Zoey gave him a look like she was trying to figure out what he was thinking, but he wasn't sure he wanted to give his theory any more air than necessary.

The last thing he wanted to do was give Zoey false hope when it came to finding her brother alive— especially given the fact they hadn't found any trace of him in the last forty-eight hours.

Eli nodded. Yes, there was no way his stupid theory was right. And besides, Chad was far from being the romantic in the family. This wasn't a case of love making life go off the rails. Instead, the faceless enemy that was gnawing at their heels had to be something different, something not quite as dangerous as love but likely far more lethal.

Chapter Fifteen

She couldn't stand the inaction. As she stared down the alley in the direction of the apartment building, she had never felt more impotent. They had to act. Now. She didn't care about the danger it would put her in. She was willing and ready to kill any jackass who stood between her and her brother.

But she couldn't put Eli or her brother in danger by being impetuous. They had to be careful, to play this smart.

At the same time, she'd never been known for being overly cautious.

She gave Eli an impish grin as she thought about their next move. "Eli, what size dress do you wear?"

"What?" Eli asked looking at her like she'd lost her mind.

"I'm serious," she said as a wave of excitement pulsed through her. "Think about it—we allowed room service to come into our hotel room without question. We didn't even think about it, or at least I didn't. If you dressed like a cleaning woman, you could probably walk right in," she teased. "You might be our best chance to get in there."

"No." He shook his head.

Zoey laughed at his obvious discomfort. "You don't want to get in touch with your feminine side?" She feigned a look of disappointment. "I always like a man who has a certain gentleness."

"I always knew that," he teased. "Especially when we were elbow deep in the blood of our enemies in Tikrit."

"Absolutely," she said with a chuckle. "There's nothing more feminine than a little spatter on your cargo shorts… Well, that is, except for you dressing up like a cleaning lady. That would make me *hot*."

He snorted in derision. "I can get you hotter than that in plenty of other ways. I don't need to lace up a corset and wear stockings to make you want me."

She paused for a moment, not quite sure what to say. He didn't seem to notice. Instead, he continued, "But if dressing up like a woman is what I need to do to get back into your good graces, then I'll do it. Strap on the Betty Boop wig." His booming laugh bounced off the walls of the buildings surrounding them like a rubber ball until it rolled to a stop at her feet.

She wasn't laughing. Rather, she was thinking of what he had said. "You think you're not in my good graces?"

His face dropped, and the smile faded from his lips. He shoved his hand in his pocket, the simple motion reminding her of a man in the midst of interrogation. "Zoey, from the moment I came back and saw you in Billings, I wanted to be back in your life. Thought I made that obvious."

She hadn't questioned that. "I know, and I appreciate your help. I really do."

"So, you're not upset with me? You know, after what happened on the plane?" He looked at her like he was just waiting for the whip to fall.

Maybe she had made a mistake in bringing this up. It would've been so much easier to just buy him a dress and let him traipse around the apartments like a cleaning woman—at least they would've been laughing. Instead, here they were once again dealing with the awkwardness that came with their relationship.

"I'm not upset with you. But I was embarrassed. I deserved being rejected by you after everything I put you through, but—"

"Stop right there." He moved closer to her. So close that she could smell the sweet scent of the nervous sweat on his skin. "What happened in the past between us—well, it can't be undone. But I would never hold a grudge against you for decisions you made back then. We were both hurting."

Pangs of love rippled through her chest, like his words were a pebble dropped into the smooth surface of a lake.

Dammit, why did he have to be so perfect? It was just too bad perfect wasn't what she wanted in her life. She needed a man who would make mistakes, just like her. It was too much pressure if he was perfect and she was always trying to be deserving of his love. She needed someone just as screwed up as her or a relationship would never work. They had been proof of that.

"Eli—"

Before she could say anything, he pressed her up against the building behind them and took her lips with his. It was so unexpected, so surprising, that she didn't know what to do. Part of her wanted to push him away, but at the same time she wanted the feeling of his lips pressed against hers and his tongue caressing the edges of her mouth like he was tasting her lips.

She closed her eyes, and let it be. Nothing else mattered.

That was, until he broke free of her kiss.

She grabbed his shirt and moved to draw him closer to her, but he stopped and looked over his shoulder. "Did you see her?" he whispered.

"See who?" she asked, momentarily forgetting everything that was happening in their lives.

"The woman from the video, Shaye." He nudged his chin in the direction of a small farmer's market that was set up to the left of where they stood.

There were at least a dozen vendors selling everything from plump, juicy-looking grapes to freshly roasted almonds. A woman passed by them, holding the hand of a young boy who was greedily stuffing bits of what must have been contraband chocolate into his mouth. He looked up at the woman, making sure she wasn't watching as he stuffed his pudgy fingers back into the pocket of his jacket and drew out another fistful of candy.

That woman could have been her...in a different life.

"There," Eli said, pulling her back, "She's at the far stand."

There, barely visible through the throngs of people who walked among the stalls was a tall woman with slender hands. She was pointing at something Zoey couldn't see. The woman was wearing face-shielding sunglasses and a checkered scarf over her hair, giving her an Audrey Hepburn–esque look.

The word *classy* came to mind. Followed on its heels was *kidnapper*, but it seemed like a word that would only be used when explaining what happened to a woman like her, not something the woman was capable of.

In a way, the woman reminded Zoey of herself, all the contrasting parts of her life. On one hand, she was capable of being so incredibly strong and resourceful, resilient in the face of extreme odds and hardship. And yet, when it came to her personal life, she was a bundle of nerves. Eli could almost bring her to her knees with the simple touch of his hand to her cheek.

Strong and sensitive...and completely unsure of herself when it came to pulling the trigger. Maybe she wasn't as much like the bureaucrat's daughter as she believed. The woman standing in front of her would probably kill in an instant.

"We have to get to that apartment," Zoey urged, spinning around on her heel and moving away from the woman.

Eli stopped her with a touch of his hand. "What if we took her?"

She stared at him, hardly able to believe his suggestion. "If we kidnap her, we are no better than them."

"It's not about who is better or who is worse. It's about keeping your brother safe. If we grab her, at least we can negotiate a trade. Right now, all we have is the vague hope of finding your brother in that building. But what if he isn't there? What if he's been moved?"

She wasn't a fan of his plan, but he made a good point. If they took her, at least they had access to whoever was holding her brother. "We don't even have a place to stay. If we grab her, what are we going to do with her?"

"Just because we had to check out of our hotel, doesn't mean we don't have a place to stay. We can figure this out." He was already moving in the direction of the woman.

She let him walk ahead of her. He feigned interest in the stalls as he meandered toward the woman in his best attempt to not look suspicious.

As they drew nearer, Zoey stopped at the fruit stand and picked up an orange. She handed the vendor some change, but didn't take her eyes off their target. Eli glanced back at her, checking her position before he advanced.

Shaye turned toward them as she completed her purchase. She dropped a few Euros into her purse, the same purse from the video. This was definitely their target, but the woman seemed almost at ease flitting through the market stalls.

Shaye drifted to the next stall and smiled at the man standing behind his table of trinkets. She picked up a keyring and inspected it.

She acted nothing like a woman holding a man hostage.

There was something wrong. Something just didn't feel right.

Eli made his way to the woman, but instead of taking her by the arm and dragging her into an alley, he stopped beside her and picked up a hand fan.

From where she stood Zoey couldn't hear what Eli was saying, but as he spoke the woman smiled.

Zoey had never been an accomplice in a kidnapping before, but she wasn't sure that smiles and laughter were supposed to be part of it. An odd sensation of jealousy crept through her as she watched the woman lean toward Eli and touch him gently on the shoulder.

Zoey glanced around, searching the crowd for anyone that appeared to be standing guard for the woman, or anything that would help her make sense of why Eli was flirting rather than grabbing her and making off like a caveman.

He had to be seeing something different than she was, something that made him use this approach. Zoey wished she had been more adamant in her refusal of kidnapping the bureaucrat's daughter.

She dug her nails into the skin of the innocent orange. Sure, it hadn't done anything to her, but it was the nearest thing to a stress ball she had.

The skin popped under her nails as she pried it loose in one complete, long peel. Dumping the peel in a bin, she popped the first bite into her mouth. The tangy citrus flavor exploded in her mouth. It tasted of the sweet, warm sunshine and dark, languid earth.

There was a forbidden quality to the acidic nectar that dotted her lips, and as she licked the flavor away, it reminded her ever so slightly of Eli's kiss… A kiss she had momentarily claimed, but had no future hold on.

Besides, it didn't make sense to listen to the gnashing, teeth-baring lioness that roared with anger within her. There was no call to be jealous. Zoey had released her claim on him and with it she had also released the right to feel anything beyond civility toward the man.

He glanced in her general direction and the smile on his lips disappeared. A thin layer of sweat appeared on his forehead, but it couldn't have been from the fall heat.

Eli said something to the woman and, taking her

hand, he escorted her toward a small café that sat at the corner of the intersection. He sat down with Shaye at a small metal bistro table and picked up the menu like they were on a midmorning date. Shaye took off her headscarf and flipped her hair back over her shoulder as she sat down with her back to Zoey.

Though they weren't close, Zoey could make out the ring of the woman's laugh as she crossed her ankles and leaned into Eli.

Enough was enough.

Unable to hold back the roaring lioness any longer, Zoey pushed her way through the crowd, garnering more than a few frowns and mumblings in Spanish from strangers, but she didn't care. Whatever he was doing, he was doing it wrong.

As she neared the table, he excused himself and headed her off, grabbing her by the arm and leading her inside the café and out of view of the woman.

"What are you doing?" he fumed, as he glanced over his shoulder in the direction of his waiting date.

"Seriously, what am *I* doing?" She glared at him.

He wrapped his hand around the back of his neck and he let go of her hand. "I couldn't just grab her off the street. How would that look—a woman kicking and screaming as I drag her away from the crowd? I don't know about you, but I don't want to end up in a Spanish prison. I don't have to kidnap a woman to keep her occupied."

"And just how do you plan to keep her occupied?" she spat. "You think she'll bring you to her apartment as her new lover?" She tried to not sound bitter, but she couldn't keep her feelings from flecking her words.

Eli reached down, took hold of her hand and gave it a light squeeze. "I don't want a *new* lover. All I want is you. You know that. Or at least you *should* know that. From the moment this all started, all I've wanted is you."

And with just a few words, she once again felt cut off at her knees.

She sucked in a long breath and followed it with an equally long exhale. "Then what are you thinking?" she asked, sidestepping around his declaration. Though it had been exactly what she had wanted him to say, she wasn't prepared to respond.

"I want you to go to this address." He slipped her a note with an address. "There you'll find a friend of mine. A guy from my Watch Dog team. He will go with you and together you can get into the apartment. I'll keep her busy."

"There is no goddamned way I'm letting you go off alone with this woman while you foist me off on some stranger." She wadded up the piece of paper and threw it on the ground.

If they were separated, there was no telling what would happen. For all they knew, the bureaucrat's daughter knew exactly who they were and Eli was walking straight into a trap.

"I'm staying right here," Zoey said. "That is, unless you are trying to get her to take you home."

His face reddened. "Actually, if you're so adamant that you won't go to the apartment without me, what better way could there be to get into her building to look around for Chad?"

Screw that. She hated the idea of them flirting their way toward the bedroom.

"Not gonna happen." She shook her head like she could shake away the image.

"You aren't jealous, are you?" he asked. "I told you how I feel about you."

She didn't want to be needy, or to make a scene, but she felt herself steadily approaching a precipice. If they were going to be a team, she was going to have to trust him. He had said he cared only for her, that he *wanted* her. It may not have been a proclamation of love and forever, but it was more than she had expected.

She bent down and picked up the address he had given her and stuffed it into her pocket. Though she had no intention of going to a stranger to get help, she would do what she had to do to ensure they all remained safe...or as safe as they could be.

"I'm not jealous," she said, feeling the weight of her lie as she forced herself to stand tall in front of him. "You go ahead, but instead of taking her back to her apartment, keep her here."

His eyebrow rose as he must have seen through her dishonesty. It wasn't pettiness, but the primal need to protect the thing she cared for most...even if that thing—rather, that *person*—was a full-grown man.

He nodded, but said nothing and instead stared at her like he was waiting for a "but." Instead, she said nothing. She would choose to trust that whatever happened in that café was for Chad's benefit.

"Do whatever you need to do to remain safe."

He opened his mouth to speak, but she stopped him with a slight shake of her head. They didn't need to talk about her unspoken meaning.

"Call my friend. His name is Frogger."

"I've got this." With that, she turned, walking out of the café and away from the faux date.

With every step it felt as if her heart were a piece of putty being stretched and pulled into a long strand that connected them wherever they went. No matter what, no matter how thin the thread became, or how immense the distance, she would never let their bond be broken.

Chapter Sixteen

The last time he had seen Zoey look that torn was the moment she had told him she was pregnant. He could feel her confusion like it was a fog that had rolled in off the sea and settled over them. It had been stupid of him to befriend the prime minister's daughter, but it was the only thing he could think of in a pinch.

He wanted to run after Zoey, to make sure that she wasn't walking out of his life again, but he stopped himself. Desperate was never a good look on anyone. She had to know that he never wanted to do anything that would compromise their burgeoning friendship. If anything, he had been the one to lay himself out there and tell her that he wanted her, and she had said…nothing.

If anyone should have been walking off, hurt by the other, it was him. He was here for her. He was always there for her. He would give everything that he owned to be with her. And she was always breaking his heart.

All he wanted, and had ever wanted, was to be hers.

He rubbed his neck as he walked back toward

Shaye. He wasn't sure how, but now he was even more at a loss than when he had chatted her up. At that moment, at least he had his best friend at his back. Now, he was alone. And he was the one who had sent Zoey away.

He was screwing it up all over again.

He sat down and forced his face to smile. "Sorry about that. I saw someone I knew from college."

"Oh, yeah," Shaye said, twisting her pearl earring. "Where did you go to school?"

"Notre Dame. In the States," he lied. He had never gone to college, not with a father like his; instead, he had been forced to go into the military or get a job.

How little he had known about the world then.

It was a stark contrast to his reality now. The only perspective that hadn't changed from his formative years was that the world was a deadly and evil place, and the scavengers were always waiting in the shadows to pick his bones clean.

"Eli?" Shaye asked, sounding as though she had asked him a question he had failed to hear.

"Sorry, what?" He forced himself to concentrate on the woman sitting across the table from him.

"Who's the woman?"

He could feel the blood rushing from his face. "Huh? What woman?" he said, trying to play dumb, but looking in the direction that Zoey had disappeared.

"You know, the woman you are thinking about?"

He sat dumbfounded, saying nothing as he stared at Shaye.

"It's okay." Her English was accented with the slightest trill, and the effect made her sound like something out of a fairy tale, nothing like the big bad wolf that they had made her out to be. "I know the look of love in a man's eyes. I have seen it many times in my life."

"It sounds like you've been incredibly lucky in love."

As she took a sip of her espresso, her hand shook, making a dribble twist down from the corner of her mouth. Her cup clanked against the plate as she put it back down and wiped the offending drop from her chin. "I suppose my success would depend on who you asked," she said daintily placing her linen napkin back in her lap.

"I must admit, when I first spotted you at the market, I thought you were incredibly beautiful and vaguely *familiar.*"

She looked at him for a long moment like she was trying to decide whether or not he knew who she was. Like Icarus, he had flown too close.

"You belong on a runway rather than sitting here with me," he added, hoping he could keep her from shutting down on him before he got the information that he needed from her or worse, leaving and going back to the apartment and compromising Zoey's position.

He had to keep Shaye here as long as he could in

order to keep the woman he loved safe. It felt strange being on a pseudo date with a bureaucrat's daughter, but thinking only about Zoey. Oh, the things he did for her.

"Actually, I'm here in Spain with a man." She picked at a piece of bread the waiter had left at the table, rolling the dough between her fingers until the bits became shaped like little grenades that she could use to destroy him.

If he had been on a real date with her and hadn't known the story behind her appearance in this marketplace, he would've been hurt that she was shooting him down.

"And who is the man?" Eli asked. "You love him?"

She tore off another piece of bread as she dropped the first doughy grenade on the table. She must have wanted to create a full arsenal.

"It doesn't matter who I love." The waiter strode over and placed a bowl of olives beside the bread.

They each gave him their order, for him paella and her a caprese salad. As the waiter strode from the table, Eli turned back to her. "If you're here with another man, why did you agree to have lunch with me?" he asked, hoping that the question would sound like a man who wanted to date her.

She looked torn, but he didn't know why. Perhaps it had something to do with Chad, and knowing that she was holding him hostage somewhere. The thought reminded Eli that regardless of how amiable the woman seemed, or how pretty her face, he was dealing with a potential killer. It was often the ones like her, women with an abundance of physical assets, who flew well above anyone's radar.

But he couldn't forget.

"I agreed to come along with you because you looked interesting." She moved slightly in her seat, turning her knees away from him as though she were closing a part of herself off.

He'd seen people use this subtle body language many times when he had been tasked with interrogating. It was the body's equivalent of saying there wasn't a chance in hell of his getting whatever information he wanted—the interrogation was over.

He had to get her to open up to him again.

"I looked interesting, huh?" He tried to give her his sexiest grin. "I'll take it."

She quirked an eyebrow. "Has anyone ever told you that you are not a humble man?"

"I hear there are worse things to be." He popped an olive into his mouth and chomped on it like it was a grain of truth.

Shaye laughed. "I'm glad I'm not in danger of falling for your charms."

"If I were a lesser man, I would be deeply hurt. However, I believe I do love a woman. You are safe from whatever charms you think I have." Eli looked down at Shaye's hands, half expecting to see something that would give away all the evil things she had done. Instead, she had the long, manicured nails of a woman who wasn't accustomed to manual labor.

These were not the hands of a woman who had cut off Chad's finger. However, just because she hadn't wielded the knife, didn't mean she wasn't the one responsible for the amputation.

"What do you think of corporal punishment?" Once again, he could feel his wings starting to melt as he neared the sun.

"Well—" She sat in stunned silence for a moment. "It appears you are far more interesting than I had initially assumed. Now, I cannot help wondering if I should have stayed far away from you. I fear you are a dangerous man." She stood up, picking up her scarf from the table and swiftly wrapping it over her hair, like a symbolic white flag.

He fell back down to earth. He stood up and threw a bit of money on the table as he moved after her. "Stop, please," he called.

She didn't even look back at him as she strode away in the direction of the apartment. Eli wasn't sure if he should go after her and grab her, as in the initial plan, or if he should simply let her go. For all he knew, Zoey was in her apartment with Chad right now. If Shaye found her there, and if Chad wasn't already dead, she would likely kill them both.

The only thing Eli could do was what he had planned in the first place.

The prime minister's daughter was about a half block from him as he started to jog after her. As she approached the end of the street, he spotted Zoey as she came out and jabbed the woman with the tip of a pen.

Clever girl.

Though they had often talked about the best methods to drug an enemy, they had never used the old Russian Cold War trick in practice—until now.

He slowed to a walk as Shaye said something to Zoey, no doubt chastising her. Undoubtedly, no one on the street had noticed what Zoey had done, except him. Zoey looked back at him as the woman crossed the street ahead of them. They likely had only minutes before the prime minister's daughter would feel any ill effects from the drug. After that, they would have to swiftly remove her from prying eyes.

As he caught up to Zoey, he couldn't help but wonder why the bureaucrat's daughter in a foreign land had not only agreed to have lunch with him, but also been devoid of any security personnel. Either she was impetuous and stupid, or her father had wanted her to disappear. Was it possible that this young girl had a contract out on her head, as well?

One thing was certain, in coming to Spain and allowing them access, the woman had made a mistake—a mistake that was to their advantage.

Chapter Seventeen

Sometimes being bad felt so good. Zoey wrapped her arm under Shaye's as the prime minister's daughter began to list forward. "Come now, Shaye, I'll take you back to your apartment. I bet my brother's waiting."

The woman looked at her through cloudy eyes, like she was trying to make sense of the words that were coming out of Zoey's mouth. "What?" Shaye asked, her speech slurred.

Eli took the woman by the other arm, and as he grabbed her, it was as if she were suddenly weightless.

"You couldn't drug her a little bit closer to her apartment?" Eli asked, sending her an approving grin.

"Well, if your Prince Charming act had worked, I wouldn't have had to drug her at all. This is really on you." Zoey glanced down the street—they were only a few buildings from the apartments.

"Look in her purse," Eli said, motioning toward the expensive bag on her arm. "We are going to need her keys to get into the building."

Careful not to let the princess fall, she rifled around in her bag until she found a key ring, complete with a small mink fur ball.

She lifted the keys with a jingle for Eli to see. "We're in like Flynn."

He cringed. "You just jinxed us. Why did you just jinx us?"

She rolled her eyes, the gesture suddenly making her feel more like the girl at Victoria's Secret. "Don't be so superstitious."

They stopped in front of the apartment building where they had last traced the GPS device. She lifted the keys, hoping it would be easy to pick which one belonged in the lock, before anyone would suspect their being there. However, as she moved closer to the glass doors, there was no area for a key, rather there was only an electronic keypad.

Crap.

Maybe she really had jinxed them. What were they going to do now?

She turned to the nearly unconscious woman. "What's your access pin?"

Shaye mumbled and her chin dropped down to her chest.

"Can you do some super tech genius thing and get us in?" Eli asked, taking hold of Shaye so Zoey could work.

She was capable of doing many things when it came to tech and breaking into tech-based security systems, but she didn't have any of her supplies. "If

I had a paperclip, a contact lens and a wad of chewing gum I might be able to do something."

Eli reached into his pocket and shuffled around. "I think I have a piece of gum in my pocket somewhere." He sounded excited, and it only made her feel bad.

"I was kidding, Eli." She gave him an apologetic smile. "Knowing this lady, though, the number is probably something stupid. It's probably a number that's always right there in her life, like a birthday or—"

"How many people she's killed," Eli said, finishing her sentence.

"If that's the case, then I hope the number is zero." She gave him a warning look, but she could tell from the look on his face what he really meant was that they could be walking into a situation where she would find her brother deceased in the girl's apartment.

Zoey didn't need a reminder.

"Do you know anything about this building?" Eli asked. "Maybe if we can pull something about the owners…" He stopped talking, like he realized he was grasping at straws.

Think, Zoey, think.

She nibbled on her lip, wishing she had brought a larger kit with her, but she hadn't anticipated breaking and entering. "Seriously, though, if we had a rare earth magnet and a sock, we could break the keypad and get in." She could hear herself sounding more and more like Eli as the nervous excitement started to swell within her. She glanced at him, but he shrugged like he didn't even know what a rare earth magnet was. "If there's a hardware store around here…" She paused. "Actually, I think I saw one near the bank."

This was doable. They could get in. They would just have to be creative.

They couldn't leave Shaye here by herself, and there was no way they could drag her through town and to the hardware store in the state she was in. If they got an Uber or a taxi, they'd have to explain their drunk friend and she wasn't sure she wanted to do that, either.

Their best bet was for her to head to the hardware store to get what she needed. And Eli could wait for her to return; or, if they got lucky, for another person who lived in the building to show up and then they could copy their access code. But there was no telling when another person would come to the building, and time was slipping by.

"Dude," Eli said, moving to the door. "I have an idea. What was the amount of that wire transfer?"

"$500,226.23. Why?"

He pressed 2-2-6-2 into the keypad. The red light flashed. He huffed. Then pressed 2-6-2-3. The green light flashed and the door's lock clicked open.

With a beaming smile, he settled Shaye against him and opened the door. "After you, my lady."

"Nicely done, MacGyver." She giggled.

Making her way inside, she glanced around the lobby of the building, making sure there were no active cameras. Luckily, it appeared this building was managed by people who honored the privacy of their renters. The door clicked shut behind them and their footfalls echoed against the stone floors. Inside the lobby was a seating area set around a crackling fire. It was cool, making her wonder if it was nothing more than show.

She pressed the only button on the elevator bank, going up. "And what about what floor to find Chad on? Did he tell you that in his mysterious wire transfer numbers, as well?" She quirked her brow playfully, thankful that Eli had gotten them the break they so desperately needed.

He made a show of pressing the button for the second floor as they got into the elevator with the unconscious Shaye. He laughed as he turned to her. "I think that's it, but honestly I have no idea if that's the right floor or not."

"Here's hoping your good luck lasts," Zoey said, crossing her fingers. The doors to the elevator bank closed, and as they ascended, Zoey's nerves began to rise, as well. She couldn't stand the thought of what would happen if she got into that room and found herself in a situation like the one they had with Trish. If there was a firefight, Zoey wasn't sure she could pull the trigger.

If she couldn't, and if one of them or Chad was hurt or killed, she would be the one who would have to tell the rest of the family. She was already on thin ice with her brothers, who were dealing with Trish's death in their own stoic ways. In fact, Chad had seemed like the only one who had been doing relatively well—at least until Trevor and Jarrod had met their fiancées.

She glanced over at Eli. He was staring up at the number near the elevator doors as it dinged to the second floor. He lifted Shaye up into his arms as they got out of the elevator, like he was cradling a small child instead of a possible killer. They walked to the only door on the floor. There was another keypad. She gave Eli a weary look as she punched in the same code, hoping it would work as well as it had last time.

There was the click and slide as the door unlocked. She wasn't sure she had ever been more grateful. All they had to do now was grab Chad, deal with Shaye and get the hell out of there.

As she touched the doorknob, moving to open it, Eli cleared his throat. She looked at him and realized that he was silently chastising her. He motioned toward the gun he knew she carried in her purse. She cringed.

They couldn't walk in there unprepared and unarmed. He was right. There was no telling who, or what they would find, and the last thing she wanted was to walk into the middle of a trap. But the thought of getting close to someone, looking them in the eye and pulling the trigger, made her stomach churn.

And that reaction made her a liability. And Eli had to have known it, too.

Zoey quietly drew the gun from her bag. She jacked the round in the chamber and drew her weapon, readying herself. Eli gave her a stiff nod. She opened the door only slightly, scanning the room for any visible threat before opening it wider so that Eli and Shaye could move through.

Inside, she could see a long hallway, and at the end of it was a set of double doors that led into what looked like a living room with books adorning the walls. There were several doors on each side of the hall that must have led to the rest of the enormous apartment. Though she didn't see anyone here, there may well have been an entire crew of people hiding throughout the complex. However, for now it appeared that they were alone.

The door was silent as she closed it behind them. Making their way deeper into the apartment, she heard the sound of a TV from inside one of the many rooms. Their footfalls sounded only slightly as they made their way down the marble hall. The apartment was sparsely decorated, as though Shaye had only just moved in or was almost done moving out. There was nothing on the walls, and there were boxes stacked here and there outside of the doors. The place must have been newly renovated as it still carried the smell of fresh paint and wood.

They crept down the hallway toward the sound of the television. Maybe Shaye had left Chad in the care of a bodyguard and they had been keeping him entertained. The fact that there was a TV on had to be a good sign—at least there weren't the subtle sounds of someone being tortured or the rat-a-tat-tat of gunfire. Things could've been so much worse.

On the other hand, it was almost a little too quiet. If her brother was here, and still alive, he would be fighting or making a plan to escape.

Martins weren't quitters. They weren't the kind of family who let others tromp all over them. And they certainly weren't the kind of people to act as quiet hostages. Her stomach tied into knots and her heartbeat was so loud in her ears that it almost sounded as if someone were beating on the closed door to her right.

Chad was going to be okay. He had to be okay. And if he wasn't okay—she glanced over at their newest acquisition and stared at her closed eyes—Shaye was going to die.

She opened her mouth, considering calling out. But she stopped herself. If there were other people in this apartment, she couldn't alert them to her presence. For now, they had the element of surprise.

She concentrated on her breathing as her body tightened, readying itself for a fight. The gun in her hands trembled ever so slightly. She had spent many hours at the range firing her Glock, but she would never get over the nerves that came with facing an adversary. She should've been the one trudging Shaye around so Eli could take point.

She turned to him. His body brushed against her as he moved to her side. Shaye's cheek was pressed against Eli's chest, just where Zoey had curled against him on the plane. That familiar sensation of jealousy crept up on her. If she closed her eyes and thought back, she could still hear the beating of his heart and could feel the hard muscles of his core as she traced her fingers over his skin.

They should have slept together. If they had, and this went all kinds of haywire, at least she could have been with him one more time.

But she couldn't focus on him right now or the way she felt. She had to leave the past in the past and focus on the hunt for her brother and hope it wouldn't end in a bloodbath.

As for Shaye, Eli could keep carrying her. As much as Zoey hated the thought of killing someone, if she needed the impetus for pulling the trigger, all she had to do was take one look at the woman in Eli's arms—she had to protect those she cared for.

"It's going to be okay," Eli whispered, almost imperceptibly, as they neared the living room.

He stopped and gently set Shaye down on the floor, her head bowing to one side as she settled against the wainscoting. As Eli stood, he pulled his gun from his holster. He didn't jack a round in the chamber, which made her wonder if he had been walking around with a live round the entire time. He was always the tough one, but he was a stickler when it came to safety. If he was strapped and loaded, then he was definitely feeling more antsy than he had let on.

There was a dating game on the television. And as they pressed against the wall near the door, a woman was chatting in English, talking about how she hated men who wore their socks to bed. She giggled as she spoke, as if drunk on the audience's attention.

Zoey smirked. If that was all the woman had to worry about, she'd clearly never been four seconds from a likely gun battle. That woman needed some perspective in her life.

Eli placed his back against the wall and pivoted into the living room. He cleared the room, covering the left side of the room as she cleared the right. There was a couch at the center of the room, facing the television.

"Get down!" Eli called, aiming his gun at the couch.

The back of the couch flexed as a man sat up and looked over the top at them. "What in the hell?" he said with a faint Spanish accent.

"Get on the ground," Eli commanded, his tone deep and threatening.

The man dropped to the ground in front of the leather couch and put his hands on the back of his head.

She side-stepped around the couch, aiming at the man's back. He was wearing a gray T-shirt, sweat-pants, and had on a black knit hat—even though it was warm in the house. There was a half-eaten bag of chips and a can of Coke on the table beside him.

"Who in the hell are you?" the guy asked, looking up from the ground. "I didn't do anything. How did you get in here?"

Zoey had been prepared for a variety of situations, but not barging in on an innocent man hanging out in his pajamas and watching TV. Had they just invaded a blameless guy's apartment? Was their assumption about Chad's location wrong? If it was, that meant they were back to square one.

"Where's Chad?" Eli asked, his voice the human equivalent of a German shepherd.

The guy looked up at them with a confused expression on his face. "Chad's back there." He nudged his chin in the direction from which they had come.

Feeling returned to Zoey's body as relief flooded through her. Chad was here. They had been right. She was going to save him. Everything was okay— or so she hoped.

"If you bastards hurt one freaking hair on his head..." Zoey started.

"You can take it up with him," the guy said, gesturing in the direction he had said her brother was being kept.

Was Chad even a hostage? The guy in his pajamas wasn't carrying a weapon. And if he was a bodyguard, he was doing a crappy job. And yet Chad had gone completely silent, which had to mean something was wrong. It was against every protocol in STEALTH to go missing and cut off all communication—silence always meant their operative was in trouble or dead.

As mad as she was at the thought of Chad being here on his own accord, she hoped that was the case, and Chad had just made a mistake in keeping quiet.

On the other hand, if that was what had happened, she was going to kill Chad herself. Really, it would be a justifiable homicide.

"Stay here with this guy. I'll go get Chad." Zoey started to move away. "Find out what this guy knows about Sleeping Beauty out there, and why she was packing one of our black market weapons."

Eli nodded, but she could tell from the pinched look on his face that he didn't like the idea.

"Don't worry, I'll be fine," she said, lifting her Glock a little higher so he knew she meant business. Though she had tried to comfort him, the look on his face remained. No matter what he thought, she was going to be okay. Even if she didn't pull the trigger, she could kick some ass.

Then again, perhaps he had seen her hands trembling when she had pulled her weapon on the attacker at the Widow Maker. He knew her demons just as well as she had once known his.

Before he could stop her, she made her way out into the hall. She stepped over Shaye's sprawled legs and around a stack of boxes.

Though she was almost certain they were nearly alone in the apartment with Chad, and her only concern was Sir Pajamas out in the living room, she was careful to be quiet as she crept to the next room. They should've cleared this whole place when they had come in, but just like the rest of this, nothing was going as planned. They were flying this operation by the seat of their pants.

She quietly clicked open the door on her right. Inside was a large chef's kitchen with stainless steel appliances and quartz countertops. Atop the stove was a single pot and spoon, and a stack of plates sat on the island. Aside from the meager assembly of dishes, the place was empty.

She stepped out and made her way to the next room, a deserted library. The empty bookshelves made the room feel gloomy. If she owned this place, they would have been filled to the brim.

Closing the door to the barren library, she wondered if Chad was even in the apartment. What if the guy had lied to get Eli alone so he could have a fighting chance instead of standing two against one? She glanced down toward the living room, but it was quiet. Hopefully Eli had everything under control.

At the end of the hall, she came to another door. She raised her gun, anticipating this room was empty like those before it. As she clicked open the door, she found herself in a man's bedroom. There was a pair of cowboy boots beside the bed and a ripped and bloodied flannel was thrown in a heap in the corner of the room. It looked like something Chad would wear.

As she stepped into the room to get a better look at the shirt, the door slipped shut behind her. As she turned, there was the sound of someone rushing toward her.

Pain erupted from her head as an object connected with the side of her face. The blow reverberated through her bones, making it sound like she had been hit by something metal. She turned slightly, but as she tried to catch sight of who or what had struck her, the world turned into a swirling mass of colors.

She tried to take control of herself and override the pain that threatened to overwhelm her. *Pain is just a signal from the body that there is something wrong*, she tried to tell herself. But the thought was as sluggish and weaving as the world around her.

Push past it. She told herself. *Focus.*

As she tried to center herself, another blow struck her from behind, making the same metallic, reverberating sound.

The swirling mass of white walls and gray bedding mixed with bright sunshine and dark shadows, becoming a vortex.

She didn't know how she found herself on the floor, but she felt the cool tiles pressed against her throbbing cheek.

Blinking, the vortex of color turned into a black hole, sucking her into its gaping maw. No matter how hard she tried to focus on the floor, she felt herself slipping deeper and deeper into the abyss. She sucked in a breath, fearing that this was it. Death had found her.

Then there was nothing.

Chapter Eighteen

What was taking Zoey so long?

Eli pulled a set of zip ties from his pack and, pressing the man's hands and feet together, hog-tied him. "What's your name?" he asked.

The man said nothing.

"Don't make me have to repeat myself." Eli pulled the zip ties tight enough that they bit into the man's wrists to act as a warning.

"You are the one standing in my living room. Don't you think I should be asking the questions?" the man said, pulling against the restraints on his wrists in a feeble attempt to free himself.

"You know," Eli said, moving to the couch and sitting, "I have yet to find myself in your position— hog-tied and forced into submission—but I think if I were you, the last thing I would be doing is acting like a smartass."

"If I get my hands on you, you will get your chance to test your theory," the man said, rolling to his side to face him.

"I highly doubt that," Eli said, picking up the remote and changing the channel off the dating show. He flipped to the news.

The last thing he needed right now was to learn more about some woman's dating preferences when he had more than enough relationship drama of his own to worry about. He had never really understood the allure of watching dating shows—they seemed fake and manipulated. But when he and Zoey had been together, he had sat through more than his fair share of them in order to make her happy.

That sacrifice, in hindsight, seemed far more real than anything a television show could come up with. For him, love was the little things…not some grand gesture.

There was the cacophony of firearms as the reporter spoke of an ongoing conflict somewhere else on the globe. Eli found that the sound was far more appealing than listening to the news. The sounds of gunfire definitely made him feel less on edge.

The guy at his feet sighed, like being on the floor was merely an annoyance instead of the life-threatening proposition Eli had intended. "Can I get you something to drink? How about a Coke?" Eli said sarcastically, motioning to the can on the table.

His inflection must've been lost on the man.

"Actually, that sounds good." The man perked up.

"Yeah, right. You can want in one hand…" Eli snarled. "In case you forgot, I'm the one sitting here with the gun. Try giving me the information I need and maybe we can get out of here. Then you can go back to watching whatever that was."

The man prickled, but Eli could see that he was trying to remain calm, though he clearly wanted to come up off the floor and deck him. "What exactly are you here for?" the man asked.

Eli wasn't sure whether or not he should say anything to the man about their true reason for being here. By now, he knew they were looking for Chad—they had said as much. But if the man didn't know about the contract out on Chad, Eli wasn't about to tell him about it.

"How did you get brought into all of this?" Eli asked. He was the one asking the questions.

The man shifted slightly on the floor, trying to find a comfortable position while they danced around one another. "I'm just here to do a job." The man paused. "You are Eli Wayne, right?"

Eli hated that the man knew who he was, and he had no idea who he was dealing with.

The man's beanie was coming off, revealing a head of red hair, the ruddy color bordering on strawberry blond. The dude looked nothing like he had any Spanish ancestry. It didn't mean he wasn't from Spain, but that and his slight Spanish accent made Eli wonder if he'd come from somewhere else—maybe even Algeria.

"I'm glad my reputation precedes me," Eli said, trying to sound far more confident than he was feeling.

He reminded himself that this man was his prisoner, not the other way around. The dude was trying to play head games with him. He couldn't allow himself to get sucked into his nonsense.

"With a reputation like yours, it's hard not to know about it," his hostage said.

"What the hell is that supposed to mean?"

So much for not pulled into his head games.

"That woman you came in with—I heard you got her pregnant…"

Eli's hands clenched and the remote in his hand cracked under the pressure. "Unless you don't want to make it out of here alive, I recommend you be *real* careful how you talk about her."

The man snorted with derision. "I heard about how she kicked you to the curb."

Who in the hell was this guy who seem to know so much about them?

Eli stood up and threw the remote on the couch. He couldn't sit here and let this man get under his skin. They needed to get Chad and get the hell out of here.

Glancing over at the man, making sure he wasn't going anywhere, Eli walked out into the hallway. Shaye was still passed out, her body tucked into the corner. They were going to need to do something about her if they stayed much longer. As he looked at her, she moved slightly as though she was starting to come around.

At the far end of the hall there was a door open, leading into a bedroom. The place was quiet and a wave of panic overtook him. Where was Zoey? She had said she was just going to get Chad. It'd been stupid of him to let her go by herself. He should've hogtied that bastard sooner and come with her to find her brother. But as he chastised himself, he thought of the look Zoey had given him, that "I don't need a man to keep me safe" expression.

She was strong, but that didn't mean she didn't need help. He tried to respect her boundaries and her desires, but no matter what she thought, everyone needed help sometimes.

He passed two closed doors as he made his way down the hall. Entering the bedroom, nothing appeared out of place. Where had she gone? He was tempted to call for her, but he stopped himself.

He moved to step back out into the hall when there was a creak in the floorboard behind him. He turned as the bedroom's closet door swung open and a man stepped out. Eli reached for his gun, but as he moved, the man pointed a yellow Taser at his chest. Eli turned to run, hoping that he could get outside of the shooting distance of the Taser before the man had a chance to pull the trigger.

It was no use.

There was the pop of the gun, the spray of confetti, and the sharp pinch of the barbs of the Taser as they bore into the skin of his ass. It felt as if he had accidentally sat on a 110-volt line. Debilitating pain coursed through him, dropping him to his knees.

Click. Click. Click. The electric current flowed through him with each sound.

A strange cry that filled the air, an odd mix between mewing and a screech, the noise like a hurt animal.

Click. Click. Click.

With the second round of clicks, Eli realized the sound was actually coming from him.

As his crying stopped, he tried to rise to his knees and get away, but found himself completely incapacitated. Then there was another round of that terrifying noise.

He had forgotten how bad this hurt. He had gone through a round of training in which they had been forced to take a hit from a Taser, then receive a round of OC spray—aka pepper spray—and then complete an obstacle course. The OC spray was the worst. Once this Taser was done pulsing, it would be over. The effects of OC spray could last for hours.

Click. Click. Click.

He could feel his heart fluttering as the electric current pulsed through every muscle in his body.

Five seconds. It would last only five seconds.

How long had he been on the ground? He prayed for this to be over. It felt like it had been going on for hours.

Had his attacker struck him with another set of barbs?

Maybe this was it. This would be how he went out. Attacked by a faceless enemy while trying to help the love of his life.

He collapsed as the pulse of electricity stopped coursing through his system.

He sucked in a breath, finally able to control his breathing again.

His body was exhausted, and as he lay there on the floor and tried to regain control of his faculties, half wondering if he'd peed himself, he noticed a set of feet across the floor. From where he lay, he could see only the soles and the sides of the brown leather shoes, but he recognized them as Zoey's.

Had she been shot with a Taser, too? Was she still alive?

He should have never let her go through the rest of the apartment alone. Why had he been so freaking stupid? Why didn't he listen to that little voice in his head that had told him she needed him? Why?

He choked on his breath, coughing and sputtering as his body flamed back to life. He had to get up. He had to get to her. Though he may have made a mistake, he had a chance now to make it right. To get her out of here. To keep her alive.

"Zoey," he called, his voice hoarse and raspy like he had taken the Taser barbs straight to the throat.

He moved to stand up, but as he struggled, there was the sound of footfalls from behind. Turning to look, he saw the quick brown flash of a man's boot as it connected with his head near the temple. There was the crunch of steel on bone and he bit his tongue, tasting the copper-rich stickiness as his body recoiled from the impact.

As bad as the Taser had been, he wished it had been the current that struck him rather than the kick. He collapsed, reality bleeding away.

Chapter Nineteen

They had walked straight into the snare. How had she not seen this coming? Getting in here had almost been too easy. She had been blinded by the hope of her brother leaving her secret messages and hints as to where to find him alive. But it could have been someone using him to get her to this point. Someone else must have known she would be searching for Chad and she would do anything to get to him.

Now, they were probably using her and Eli as bait. Hopefully they intended on keeping them alive. Bayural and his men were likely behind this. Just like them, he must've heard about the contract out on Chad's head. Using that knowledge, he must have set up this elaborate ruse, hoping it would flush them out of hiding.

At least she had told her brothers and their fiancées to stay away so the Gray Wolves wouldn't get the chance to kill them all in one fell swoop.

Zoey looked across the room at the bloodied and battered Eli. From where she lay on the floor, pretending to be passed out, she could make out the subtle rise and fall of Eli's chest. The man in the brown boots kicked him again. She wanted to jump up and pummel the man for hurting Eli, but knew it was no use. In the state that she was in, it would have been irrational to make a move.

Though she could kick some ass when necessary, with Eli out of the game she wouldn't stand a chance of making it out of here. Even if she did manage to somehow take down the man who had just taken both her and Eli out, there was no way she would leave Eli behind. For all she knew, their enemies could be hiding out in the apartment. The man turned on the heel of his boot, and as he moved Zoey shut her eyes.

Playing possum was her only defense. Even with that, the man may well choose to come over here and continue beating her. If he did, she would have to fight. She'd have to get up. She might even have to kill the man. Summoning what strength she had left, she vowed to do whatever she had to do to stay alive.

The man said something in Spanish she couldn't understand, but it sounded like expletives.

Good. At least he was as pissed off as she was. She would have hated it if taking them down had been easy on the man.

She wished she had put up more of a fight, but even now, as she forced her eyes to stay closed, there was a throbbing in her head. With each throb, a burst of light filled her darkened vision. *Boom. Boom. Boom.*

The sound reminded her of the clicks she had awoken to.

The sound of the Taser and Eli's cry was something she was never going to forget. Though without it, she wasn't sure whether or not she would have regained consciousness.

The man's footsteps moved toward the door and then it slammed shut. There was a click of a lock.

His footfalls cascaded down the hall as the man yelled something.

With the sounds of his voice growing more distant, Zoey was tempted to open her eyes and go check on Eli. Before she did, she held her breath and listened for anyone else in the room. She had only seen the one man who had taken her down—the bastard in the boots—but that didn't mean there wasn't someone else.

The only sound she heard was the slow, methodical breathing of Eli.

Thank all that was good he was alive.

She would have to try her damnedest to keep it that way.

Zoey peeked out from beneath her eyelashes. Eli wasn't moving, but there was a rigidity in his body that made her wonder if he was faking unconsciousness.

"Eli?" she whispered. "You okay?"

He didn't answer.

She must have seen something that wasn't truly there. She scooted her body across the floor and as she moved, the thundering in her head amplified. In all likelihood she had a concussion, but there was nothing she could do about it now. All she could focus on was the here and now, and getting them both to safety.

She leaned over Eli. He smelled of sweat and pain. Running her fingers through his hair, she tried to comfort him and draw him back to the present. "Eli, come back to me. Baby, I need you. Please," she cooed, but as she spoke, her voice cracked with emotion.

She swallowed back the feelings that betrayed her. She needed unwavering strength.

Eli's eyelids fluttered and a cute half grin peppered his face. "I need you, too."

She leaned in and kissed Eli's soft lips. As they fell into one another, a tear slipped down her cheek.

He was okay. They were together.

They could get out of this place alive.

She hoped.

Reaching up, Eli cupped her face and wiped away the tear on her cheek with his thumb. "You don't need to worry. I've got you, honey. I've always got you." He sat up and wrapped his arms around her.

In that moment, blanketed in his warm touch, she felt comfort. Their lives were in danger, and the world threatened to come crashing down on them, but she had fallen into the safety and security of the only man she had ever truly loved.

Though many things had turned her heart cold

in the past, sitting here in his arms her heart was re-awakened. They may never make it out of this room, but she finally truly had come back to her center—and to her home—in his arms.

If she lived or died, at least in this one moment she was nearly complete.

At the same time, though, there was no question of whether she loved him. She couldn't tell him—not now and probably not ever. To tell him how she felt was to put him in even further danger. If she opened herself up to him and then something happened to her, it would only hold him back. If he was the only one to make it out of this room alive, she wanted him to move into the future with an open heart…a heart that was free to find love and a life that brought him joy—even if that life wasn't with her.

She took a breath, absorbing everything she could about him, from the sound of his heart, to the heat of his touch, to the subtle scent of his cologne mixed with sweat. If this was the last time she found herself in his arms, she had to remember it all.

Dusk had started to settle on the world outside their barred window. Soon, night would be upon them and with that, a sense of foreboding.

Eli moved to stand, his feet unsteady beneath him. He extended his hand to help her to her feet. Taking his proffered hand, she stood. The throbbing in her head had subsided with each second she'd stayed in his arms.

"You check the window." He motioned toward it as he stepped toward the door.

He pressed his ear against the wood, listening for any sign that they were being monitored. Then, seeming confident that they were safe, he twisted the door handle. It made a *chunk* sound as if it were locked from the outside.

"Dammit," he said. The window provided no escape, either. In addition to being barred, it had been painted shut likely decades ago. Their assailants had chosen this room well.

"Did you see any sign of Chad when you looked around the apartment?" he asked.

"I saw a shirt with blood on it, but I couldn't tell if it was his." She walked over to the corner of the room to the flannel shirt. Pinching its sleeve in a place that wasn't stained with blood, she lifted it. It was an extra-large. She wasn't sure, but she could have sworn Chad wore a medium. Even if that were true, it didn't stop her from thinking the worst.

"Do you think this was what he was wearing when they cut off his finger?" Her voice sounded tinny and foreign, like it was coming from someone else. She dropped the shirt.

Eli shrugged. "We don't know anything for sure yet. Don't worry. I'm sure he's fine."

He was lying, but she appreciated that he was making an attempt to lessen her panic.

Eli patted his pockets until he found his phone.

It was ridiculous, but for a moment she hoped he

was calling someone to help. But who was there to call? They were here in Spain alone, and their closest ally was her family in Sweden. It would take them at least half a day to get to them. By then, she and Eli were likely to be killed.

Besides, the last people they could call was her family. If the Turkish terrorist group was behind their abduction, then they couldn't risk getting all of her family together in one place. Actually, it didn't even matter who had set them up to walk into this trap. They couldn't allow her family to follow suit.

She remembered Eli's team member—the one he'd asked her to find before coming here.

"Are you going to call Watch Dog?" she asked, pulling her own phone from her pocket.

At some point the screen had been cracked, most likely when she had fallen to the floor or perhaps when the man had kicked her while she had been down.

"Yeah, Frogger is nearby." Eli tapped on the screen. "He can put together a team and extricate us before morning, I'm sure."

Though she was relieved that they had an exit strategy, she wasn't sure how it would look that another team was going to bring them to safety. If it got out that Watch Dogs had saved her, a member of STEALTH, her family's company would lose their hard-nosed edge in the contractor market.

But what did it really matter, as long as they made it out alive?

Ego didn't have a place when it came to life and death.

Watch Dog could have this victory. She would even send them a gift basket. Maybe something from their new line of tactical wear.

She chuckled at the thought.

Eli glanced over at her and furrowed his brow. "What's so funny?"

Checking her smile, she stopped, but not before glancing at his blue button-up. "Nothing. I must be tired."

She turned back to her phone and texted Jarrod an encrypted message.

Eli and I have a situation here in Spain. Going to call in Watch Dog. You all need to stay away. We will get out of this. But in case we don't, give my little Anya and the rest of the family hugs for me. Love you all.

After she hit Send, she turned off her phone, hoping to save the battery and, admittedly, she wasn't sure she wanted to see her brother's response. No doubt he would flip out.

Hopefully everything would turn out all right and soon they would all be back home at the ranch, out of danger and celebrating the holidays.

She closed her eyes and thought of it now. In her fantasy Christmas, Eli was sitting next to her opening presents as they drank eggnog and laughed about all the trouble they had found this year. They would talk about Trish and how, when she was young, she had loved *Teenage Mutant Ninja Turtles*. Michelangelo had always been her favorite.

And this was the first year they were going to get the chance to spend Christmas with Anya. Though she had only just recently entered their lives, she had changed everything. That girl was incredible. She had an extra chromosome, which made her extra in every way—and none more than her ability to bring joy to the family. She was the light in everyone's eyes. One minute around Anya and it was easy to forget your troubles and just enjoy the moment. She was the linchpin that kept every one of them grounded and centered. She needed them just as much as they needed her.

The thought of everyone made Zoey ache with longing.

She and Eli should have never come here. They should have just waited until they had found more evidence about Chad's location. They should have played it smart. But no, she had been in such a damned rush to get to him that she had brushed their rules and protocols to the side.

Now it was not only going to cost her, but it was going to cost Eli everything, as well.

There was the sound of men talking from outside the door, and she and Eli stopped moving. They both slipped their phones away.

Her heart skipped a beat with the turn of the doorknob.

"We need to kill them."

"No," the second man said, his voice thick with an accent that she couldn't place. "We need them at least until Chad arrives. Then you can kill them for all I care."

She felt the blood rush from her face and she sank down onto the edge of the bed that sat at the center of the room.

"As long as Chad *thinks* they are here, we're covered," the second man continued. "If we keep them alive, they are nothing more than a liability."

"I said no," the first man growled. "If we kill them and Chad somehow finds out, we will be back to having nothing. We need them as leverage. That's an order."

Were these men military? They had to have some sort of hierarchy. Maybe they were operatives just like them.

She choked on the urge to cry. It was nothing more than frustration, she reminded herself. That was all. She just had to keep from losing her cool and everything would be okay.

The second man let loose a string of expletives at the man's refusal. Yeah, maybe they weren't military after all, but it didn't eliminate the likelihood that they were contractors. Which meant they were looking to score the bounty on Chad's head.

"Just leave them for tonight. Tomorrow, if we haven't heard back from him, we will kill them," the first man said.

She could almost hear her clock ticking down to zero hour.

As their footfalls moved away from the door, she looked around the room for anything that could help them get out of there. The window bars refused to budge and there were no grates or openings in the floor or ceiling large enough for them to slip through. All they had were their cell phones and their wits.

"Tell your guy we're going to need him here sooner rather than later," she said, turning back to Eli, who was currently staring at his phone.

"Already done." Eli sighed. "But he's not at the address I gave you. He's traveling—and still a ways out. Until then, he told us to stay put."

She laughed at the idea that they had any other option.

Her headache worsened and she lay down on the bed, pulling up the down comforter around her tired body.

Eli dropped the phone onto the floor beside the bed and moved in next to her. "I'm sorry I got us in this mess," he said.

"What?" she said, sitting up slightly so she could look him in the eye. "You aren't the one who went all gung ho into this. If I would've stopped to think for more than three seconds, and not let my emotions get away from me, we wouldn't be here. This is all my fault. Not yours."

"Yours weren't the only choices made. We did this together. This isn't just on you."

It was strange, but she felt a bit stripped of her strength by him taking some of the blame. She wasn't sure that she liked the sensation. She deserved to feel responsible for all the bad things that were coming their way after all she had put Eli through.

He motioned for her to fold into his arms. "You don't get to carry the burden of guilt all by yourself, my love," he added.

She laid her head against him, finding comfort in the melodic rise and fall of his chest. *My love*, he had said. Was that his hint that he was falling for her again?

She ran her fingers over the buttons of his shirt and made small swirls on the fabric. This, being with him in bed, was something she had missed after they had gone their separate ways. Was she ready to open her heart up and let this happen——if they got out of here alive?

He kissed the top of her head and drew in a long breath. "You know I love you, don't you?" he whispered into her hair.

Her entire body tightened. It wasn't that she didn't want to hear those words, it was just that they came as a surprise. Sure, there were feelings between them, but love? Maybe he meant the kind of *comfortable* love that came with time and two people who became accustomed to one another.

Just because he said he loved her, it didn't mean his feelings were a *romantic* love, the kind for which people sacrificed and gave everything they had for the other: sleep, money, time, opinions and even habits...

He was certainly sacrificing everything he had for her right now.

She wanted to tell him that she loved him, too. But she had to stick to her guns. She couldn't get them out of their predicament, so the best thing she could do to protect him was to keep the truth away from him. At least until they were on the outside. But that didn't mean she couldn't take this chance to show him how she felt.

This was their night...their one last chance together. For all she knew, it could be their final goodbye. And if all they had were these few, precious hours, she was going to make the most of it.

She gazed up at him and gave him the look that had always been her cue to make love. In their past life, she had given him this look what must've been thousands of times, but none of them felt as important as this moment. This last moment.

She regretted all the mistakes she had made when it came to him. "Eli, I'm so sorry. I'm sorry I left you back then." The lump formed in her throat and she tried to swallow it back, but it refused to budge. "I never wanted to break your heart. But after we lost the baby...it changed me."

He tightened under her, but said nothing.

"Every time I closed my eyes, all I saw were the swirls of her dark brown hair—your hair. And her big green eyes—she had your eyes. And that sweet little pointed nose—she had my nose." She swallowed back the lump in her throat. "I never knew I could know such love and such heartache all at the same time."

"She was beautiful, just like her mommy." Eli ran his fingers through her hair, comforting her. "When she died, so did a piece of me... And then when you split, the rest of me withered away."

"I'm so sorry." Her voice was raspy with unshed tears. "I felt like I wasn't myself anymore. I was just a shell. But I feared that if I stayed, I would be constantly reminded of the future we could have had, just by looking in your eyes—her eyes."

He nodded, but was silent for a long moment. "You weren't the only one hurting, Zoey."

"I know." She wished she could go back in time and correct her wrongs. "And I also know that no amount of apologizing will ever be enough." She put her hand over his heart. "I was so myopic. All I could do was concentrate on my own pain and agony. I just shut down."

"Do you know that when you disappeared, I didn't stop looking for you until I knew where you had gone and that you were safe?"

She hadn't thought of the days after she had left him and run to a cabin in the Rockies in a long time. She had holed up for nearly six months. She'd only let Trish know where she was, so they wouldn't come looking for her.

Once in a while, her sister would bring her food

and check on her to make sure she was still alive; but beyond that Zoey had seen no one. Even with Trish, she had barely spoken a word, but her sister hadn't forced her to make conversation. Instead, Trish had just talked to her about what the family was working on, and assignments that they had taken.

The only thing Zoey had been capable of doing was continuing her drone strikes and IT work—which she did with manic diligence.

"Did Trish tell you where I was?" she asked.

Eli gave her a guilty look. "She knew how concerned I was about your safety." He drew in a long breath.

"Just so you know, if I could go back in time and make things right, I would. I would never run away from you like that again… No matter how badly our hearts get broken by the world." She moved atop him, straddling her legs around him.

He slipped her fingers between his and raised her hands so she was kneeling over him. He reached up and kissed her lips. In his kiss was a deep sadness and an equally deep well of desire.

"Make me a promise…" he said, his breath caressing her lips. "And we can start over, no guilt."

"What?" she asked, her voice as smooth and supplicating as his touch.

"Promise me that if we make it out of here alive, we can quit screwing around."

She smiled as she kissed his lips. "And what is that supposed to mean?"

"Let's get married."

She stopped moving and stared into his emerald eyes. He was being serious. A gust of joy breezed throughout her body. She wanted to say yes, a thousand times yes, but she stopped herself from getting too excited.

Though she feared her own demise, and what it would do if she told Eli the truth, he was going to hurt either way. He *loved* her. He wanted to *marry* her.

If she agreed, they could revel in the joy that came with promises of forever—at least for one night.

"Yes, Eli." As she answered, she realized she had never told him that she loved him, but he didn't seem to care. It was almost as if she didn't have to put words to her feelings as he already knew how she felt.

He took hold of her and pulled her down hard, his lips crushing against hers in his excitement.

Whether she ever had the chance to tell him or not, she loved this man. She would love him until the end of time and then probably even long after. He was hers and she was his, and she never wanted it any other way.

He pushed up her shirt and lifted it over her head, exposing her naked breasts. He cupped them in his hands as he sat up and moved to take her nipple in his mouth. She savored the feel of his mouth on her and how he tenderly thrilled his tongue against her sensitive nub.

She bit back a moan.

They would have to be quiet. Silent even, in their lovemaking. Their silence, mixed with the threat of danger, swirled together into a heady elixir of desire.

She hurried, taking off his pants and his shirt; stripping him of all of his underclothes in her rush to feel him.

This was it, their last moments together. This was the only future they were promised.

She kissed him, trailing her mouth down his chest until she found him. He tilted his head back into the pillow and she could hear his breath quicken as she swirled her mouth around him.

"Zoey," he said as she tasted him. "I want you. I've wanted you every moment…of every day…" His voice was faint, slipping into the euphoria.

She would be lying if she tried to tell him that it had been any different for her.

He was her everything, just as he always had been.

His body grew harder and impossibly harder as she played.

"Come here," he said, calling her to move atop him. "I need to feel you. I've missed you for so long."

She moved over him, slipping him into her gently as she rocked her hips back and forth. Their movement was easy and unrushed, as if they were both savoring the limited time they had together, and every thrust, every circle and nudge of her hips was a day they had been apart.

Their lips met as he sat up and pulled her into his lap, their knees pointing toward the ceiling. As he drove deeper and deeper into her, she thought of how much time she had missed by making one stupid decision and running away.

At least for this one day, this one moment, they could have the past that she had so foolishly stripped away.

Her breathing quickened, and she tried to force her body to listen to her mind. She wanted this moment to last—she couldn't let herself go. Not yet. But he felt so good. Being in his arms. Feeling him inside of her.

She buried her face into his neck in order to try and quiet her throaty moan as her body released, giving in to the ecstasy of being with him.

As she collected herself, she started to move again. This time, just for him.

Tonight, they would have everything the other offered—love above all.

Chapter Twenty

The next morning, before dawn, the door to their bedroom flew open. Zoey pulled herself out of Eli's arms, afraid that if their enemies saw them together they would know the most effective way to hurt her. Pajama dude was still wearing the beanie from the night before, but instead of looking bored and confused by their presence, now he looked pissed off.

"Get in there," he ordered, shoving Shaye into the room with them.

She turned back as soon as he threw her inside. "No. These people will kill me. You can't put me in here with them," she pleaded to the man as he slammed the door shut.

There was the click of the lock. Shaye screamed after the man. "Come back! No! This is absolutely unacceptable. Just wait until my father hears about what you have done." She stopped for a moment as she stared at the door. "You will be dead before nightfall!"

Ever so slowly, she turned around to face them,

a look of disgust and anger burned across her beautiful face.

"What in the hell are you doing in here?" Zoey asked, staring daggers at her.

She was definitely the kind of woman that Chad would go for. She was curvy and there was a dimple in her chin. Her long blond hair was free and falling in loose waves over her shoulders. Zoey hadn't noticed before, but the woman had eyes the color of blue glacial ice. As angry as she was, Zoey was surprised that the heat of her stare didn't cause the icy color to melt and become the hot orange hue of flames. Fire and ice... Chad's MO when it came to the women he had dated in the past.

Zoey wanted to get up and shake her to get the answers they so desperately needed, but at the same time she wasn't sure approaching the Algerian snow beast was the best option. She looked as though she was ready to scratch their eyes out.

The woman must have been put in here to act as a spy. This was her apartment and they were her men—weren't they?

As Zoey sat up, she straightened out her shirt. Luckily, both she and Eli had slipped back into their clothes after they had made love. She drew in a long breath as her thoughts drifted back to last night.

She loved the fact that his scent still perfumed her skin.

It was just a pity that she had to spend the afterglow with the woman who had been enemy number one for the last week.

"If you lay one finger on me, you will be added to *his* list," Shaye said, indicating the closed door and the men outside.

"We have no intention of doing anything of the sort," Eli said.

Zoey wanted to tell him to speak for himself— she was more than willing to take this woman down if it led to Chad.

"Is that right?" Shaye spat, pulling her hair back like she wanted to put it up, but stopped as she must have realized it was a nervous tic that made her look weaker. "Is that why you drugged me and forced me to come back here?"

Forced her? "Isn't this your apartment?" Zoey asked. Eli set his hand on her thigh, a subtle reminder that they had to be careful about what they did and didn't say.

She needed no reminding.

"It's my friend's apartment, but I had no intention of coming back after—" She went silent.

"After what?" Eli asked, his voice taking on a soft, caring tone that Zoey couldn't have conjured even for all the wealth in the world.

Shaye walked across the room and stared out the window, suddenly acting like she couldn't hear them.

"Is my brother Chad still alive?"

"He's your *brother*?" Shaye asked, turning with a start. "Odd."

Her surprise made Zoey wonder if her and Chad's relationship wasn't what she had assumed. If Chad was dating this woman, he wouldn't hesitate to tell her about his siblings—though none of them were normally particularly forthcoming about the family business.

"Yes. Now, is he alive?" she asked, trying hard not to grit her teeth.

"As far as I know. Why wouldn't he be?" Some of the anger seemed to drift out of Shaye's features. "What in the hell is going on?"

"We wanted to ask you the same thing," Eli said.

The woman sat down on the window's ledge, giving one more forlorn glance at the bars before looking back at them. "I don't know who you really are, or how you found me, but even if you hadn't drugged me, I wouldn't have anything to say to you."

Zoey moved to stand up, but Eli shook his head almost imperceptibly. Instead, he rose to his feet. He must have known she was close to losing her cool.

"Look," Eli said, meandering over toward her like she was a stray cat who might run away if he moved too quickly. "We didn't want to drug you. All we wanted to do was—"

"Pick me up," she said, staring at him.

"No, I just wanted to get to the bottom of a few things. And to find Chad. We know he was here… with you. We saw you together." Eli stopped about halfway to her and crossed his arms over his chest.

Her eyebrows rose and she mumbled something

unintelligible under her breath. "Your brother was fine when I left him yesterday. He was supposed to meet me at the Maricel Museum, but he never showed up."

"A museum?" Zoey asked before thinking. "He wasn't your hostage?"

"What?" Shaye scoffed. "No. Of course not. Why would you think I... Wait. Is that what all your nonsense was about? You thought I'd *kidnapped* Chad so you kidnapped me?" She gave a disbelieving shake of her head. "Americans."

Ignoring her disdain, Zoey tried to collect her thoughts. "If you didn't kidnap him and take him hostage, then what were you doing with my brother?"

"He was working for me," she said, but there was a bit of color in her cheeks.

"Doing what?" Eli asked, moving to the wall on the other side of the window from Shaye.

Shaye tapped her perfectly manicured nails against the windowsill. "Is she the woman you were thinking about when we were at the café?" She motioned toward Zoey.

Eli smiled and gave a nod. "Yes. That obvious, huh?"

The remaining anger disappeared from Shaye's face. "Even if I hadn't seen you sitting in bed with one another." Shaye blushed ever so slightly. "How long have you been together?"

Eli shifted his weight. "On and off for a few years now."

Zoey just wished she knew if it was going to be on or off when they walked out of this room—or rather, *if* they walked out of this room. In the light of day his marriage proposal last night seemed absurd. Had he really been serious?

"You said you were here with a man. Were you talking about a boyfriend or Chad?" Eli asked.

Shaye sighed. "I don't have a boyfriend. At least, not anymore."

"Did you hire Chad to kill him?" Zoey asked. It sounded odd when it escaped her lips, but what else would the woman have hired him for?

Shaye laughed. "No. Hardly. But my ex is the reason we had to leave Algeria."

The sounds of men yelling came from outside the bedroom, and they all went deathly silent. There was a tirade of obscenities coming from the other room, but she couldn't quite make out what they were fighting about. It likely had something to do with how to handle their hostages.

"Is that why your father put out a contract on Chad's head?" Zoey asked in a whisper, hoping to get as much information from the woman before the door opened and shots were fired. "Because he was involved with your ex?"

Shaye shook her head. "My father had my ex murdered about six months ago when he learned that we were thinking about getting engaged. I can't prove it, but my father hated him."

"What's your ex's name?" Zoey asked, pulling out her phone and turning it on.

"Raj Assaf. He was a fisherman's son, and my father thought he wasn't good enough for me. I didn't care what he thought. I used to think I had the right to love who I wanted. My father taught me otherwise." Shaye cupped her hands over her face as if by covering her mouth she could make the words she had just said disappear.

Zoey went to work researching the man's name. In a matter of moments, she had pulled up the contract released for the man's death. Again, it carried the mark of the black star. And though she couldn't find out the source of the contract, the language was similar to her brother's hit.

Shaye was telling the truth, and likely right about her father.

"How did Chad get dragged into all of this? What did you hire him for?" Zoey asked, dropping her phone into her lap.

"He was friends with Raj. When I told him about what had happened, he said he would be happy to kill my father to avenge his death." She looked down at her hands. "He and Raj had talked just a day before he was killed. I think your brother felt guilty about not knowing about the hit and not being able to save him."

"So, basically, you hired Chad to kill your father?" Eli asked.

"No," she said, shaking her head. "After Raj's

death, my father found a man he thought was a better match and he and the man's parents arranged for us to wed. I met him. We went to coffee. While we were there, he was texting other women. When I asked him about it, he told me that he never intended on a "true" marriage. For him, when we wed, it would be nothing more than a business arrangement. My father had even agreed to give him a job in his counsel for my dowry."

Zoey hadn't seen anything online about the arranged marriage. Just that she and her sisters were single.

"I don't want my father to die," Shaye continued. "He's old-fashioned and a bit chauvinistic, but I don't want him dead. I just want him to see that I'm my own woman. That I should be trusted to make my own decisions, and can't be treated as chattel. So, I hired Chad to kill Sami, the man I was supposed to marry."

The men outside stopped yelling and there was the sound of furniture being moved about in another room.

"Why didn't you just tell your father or Sami that you didn't want to get married? Jumping to murder seems a bit drastic," Zoey said, slipping her feet out of bed and putting on her shoes.

"I tried. Neither would hear of it. I turned to Sami's mother and father but even they dismissed my wishes—they told me marriage has never been anything other than a business transaction. For me to think otherwise was foolish." Shaye's voice was strong but laced with pain.

Zoey could understand the extreme measures. If she had ever found herself in that situation, she would have made the same choice. She couldn't even stomach the thought of what the future would bring for a woman placed in such a situation. What of love? Freedom? Choices? And what about having children with a man who treated her as nothing more than a way to get ahead?

The thought revolted her.

"Did Chad get it done?" Zoey asked, half wondering if she needed to assign the hit to someone else on her team.

She shook her head. "He tried, but Sami caught wind of my plan. My father was furious."

"And that was why he put the hit out on Chad," Eli said, finishing her thought.

Shaye stared at him. "So, he did it, then? My father ordered him killed? He had threatened, but…"

Zoey nodded.

"I'm so sorry." Shaye put her head in her hands. "I should never have brought Chad into this. He is just someone I knew I could trust. That I liked. Someone who knew Raj and wanted revenge as badly as I did."

Zoey knew all about feeling inadequate. It was the one thing she was good at.

"Chad knows the risks he faces anytime he takes a job," Zoey said, trying to comfort her. "The only mistake he made was not letting his family in on his plans."

"He mentioned that he was taking the job on the down low. I think he didn't want anyone telling him it was a bad idea. Something about keeping a low profile, but he didn't elaborate."

Chad had been right. She would have never signed off on this. Not with everything going on with the Gray Wolves.

On the other hand, she, too, had gone against her better judgment when she went to the trade show. Maybe they had all gotten a little bit too comfortable with being in danger.

The yelling started again outside the room. This time she could make out something about Chad. She listened harder, but had a hard time understanding the broken Spanish jargon the men were using.

Zoey ran her fingers through her hair, trying to pull the rat's nests out. It was far easier to untangle a days' worth of unbrushed hair than it was to untangle her brother's affairs. As she worked her fingers through her hair, she glanced over at Eli. He looked nothing like the wreck she was sure she was.

"What about these guys?" Eli asked. "Are they part of your father's crew?"

She shook her head. "My father made it clear that I'm not welcome back until I'm ready to marry Sami. If I don't return, I will be stripped of everything."

"So, you are going to go back?" Zoey asked pensively.

"Absolutely not. I have everything I need to survive. I don't need my father's wealth or his taking control of my life."

"Then were these men sent here to bring you back against your will?"

"My father wouldn't allow this." She lifted up the sleeve of her shirt, exposing a large ripening bruise. "He would never agree with them treating me like this."

Apparently, a contractor being physically aggressive to his daughter was too much for the prime minister to accept, but purchasing a groom who didn't care about his daughter was just fine.

Zoey shook her head in disbelief. "So your father didn't put out the contract on Chad?"

Shaye shrugged. "He may have, but if so, his plans have gone off the rails. These people, whoever are holding us, they will be made to pay for raising a hand against me."

Zoey phone pinged from her lap.

There was a flurry of texts from her family as her phone picked up its messages after restarting. The first she read were from Jarrod, time-stamped throughout the night.

How are you doing?

Are you okay? Text me.

We are catching a flight to get to you now.

Calling in reinforcements.

Chad still MIA. We will find him.

Get out of there.

Text us.

We're worried.

The texts from her brother went on and on, and were followed by many just like it from Trevor. At the bottom of the list of people texting her, she found Mindy's notes. Most mirrored her brother's sentiments, but the last stood out. It read:

Severed fingerprint scanned and matched to CIA database. Belongs to one Demetri Johnson. Know him?

She had no idea who that was and as she pulled up records on the man, no one with that name looked or sounded familiar.

"My family is freaking out. I think they're on their way here." Zoey looked up at Eli. "Have you gotten an update from your people at Watch Dogs? They coming soon?".

Eli glanced down at his phone and tapped a few buttons. "Radio silence. So far as I know, my buddy should have been here by now."

"Okay." As Zoey spoke, she wondered why his team was running late in extricating them. STEALTH worked nothing like that. If they made a plan for extraction, they had it planned to the second a door opened. "It sounds like my brothers are looking into Chad's disappearance. Do you have any idea where he would have gone, Shaye?"

She shook her head. "He's always been really good about being on time and being where he says he is going to be. All I can think is that these guys must've also gotten him."

"No," Eli said. "They're looking for him, too. That's the only reason we're still alive. They're using us as bait to entice Chad back here."

Who in the hell were these guys who were keeping them prisoner?

"Have you ever heard of Demetri Johnson?" Zoey asked them.

Eli blanched. "Why? What happened to him? Is he okay?"

He sounded worried, which concerned her. She didn't want to be the one to tell him what her brother's fiancée had told her.

"He is the owner of the finger we found in a hotel room," she said.

"You found a *finger*?" Shaye asked.

"Yes," Eli said. "And hopefully the man it belongs to is still alive. As it is, I think we have bigger problems than we anticipated."

"Why? Who is he?" Zoey asked.

Ell looked at her, and the expression on his face made her blood run cold. "Demetri is my friend. His call sign is Frogger. I've been talking to him ever since Billings. He was the man from Watch Dogs who I have been working with. If he's been brought into this, it could only mean one thing… My bosses have been spying on us, and they used him to send me a message. They know I've gone rogue." He paused. "I fear my involvement in this situation has been compromised and I have brought hell to our doorstep."

Chapter Twenty-One

Frogger had to be dead. And what was worse, their employer was likely behind it. He had been warned, and so had Frogger, that they were never to move against Watch Dogs. He had been crazy to think they wouldn't act against him for going rogue when it came to Chad's contract. They must've been following him every step of the way.

He was the reason they were stuck in this apartment. He was the reason they were likely going to die. And it was all because he had gotten involved in Zoey's life.

And he had to tell Zoey the truth. She was going to hate him. As it was, up until last night, she had been on the fence about ever getting close to him again. Finally, they had a breakthrough, and now here they were…going back to square one.

Crap.

"I'm so sorry, Zoey. I had no idea this was going to happen. I thought my new bosses were more like you guys. I thought that they had honor. Turns out, they're all about the money." He moved over to her and sat down beside her on the bed. Lacing his fingers through hers, he gave them a light squeeze as he stared down at the space where their skin touched.

He would hate himself forever if this was the last time he got to touch her.

Zoey sat in silence for a long moment. Shaye squirmed as she gazed out the window.

Finally, Zoey cleared her throat. "Eli, this was never going to be a mission that was cut-and-dried. You and I both know sometimes things don't go as we plan. Everything we've ever done together we've done to the best of our abilities. Well, except, *you know*... If I had done things differently during the pregnancy and then just dealt with things when it all went wrong, maybe life would've been different."

The last thing he wanted was for her to feel guilty or bad for what had happened. It hadn't been her fault. Their baby girl had just not been meant to grow up in their lives. If anything, she had been sent to become their guardian angel. And as much as he had always thought of her loss as a curse, looking at it from this perspective, maybe she had really been the greatest gift they had ever been given.

Life always had a way of self-correcting. Nothing could take away the pain and loss they had gone through, but time had proven they were better as a team.

Eli jumped up from the bed as footfalls, like that of someone running, came from outside the bedroom door. He stood with his back against the wall beside the door, grabbing the only thing that was close to him—a small bedside table.

The door flew open, smashing against the wall. There was a barrel of a gun, pointing directly at Zoey. Before he could even think, Eli swung the table. It hit with a crack and smattering of splintered wood as it connected with the beanie man's face.

He dropped to the ground with a yelp of pain. Blood poured from a gash near his eye. Though the table was in pieces, Eli swung again, hitting the man in the back of the head over and over until all Eli was holding were two broken legs and the beanie the man had been wearing was coated with blood.

Zoey ran over and picked up the man's gun. With a click, she checked to make sure it was loaded. "Let's go," she said, motioning for Shaye to follow them.

Eli took the lead and they rushed down the hall. A second man, tall and muscular, stepped out of the living room. He looked frazzled, like he was running from something and had no idea he was about to come upon them.

As he spotted Eli, he drew his weapon. But before Eli could react, a shot rippled through the air.

It whizzed toward him, striking him at full force in the chest. He looked down where the bullet had hit him. Blood seeped through the blue fabric, and he struggled to breathe, but the bullet hadn't penetrated through the shirt.

"Dang. That's going to leave a mark," he said, wheezing.

There was the boom of another shot. Eli looked up just in time to see the man who had shot him crumple to his knees. He looked surprised as his body thumped forward, his face hitting the floor.

In all the years Eli and Zoey had been together, he had never seen her pull the trigger. As he looked over at her, she stood calm, still aiming the gun at the fallen man.

She had just killed a guy, at close range, for him. If that wasn't love, he didn't know what was.

He gently pulled the gun from her hands, and she didn't fight it. "Thank you, Zoey. I've got it from here."

From the voices they had heard, there had to be at least one more man in the apartment. They had to kill him.

He quietly cleared the rooms they passed before getting to the man Zoey had shot. Blood had started to pool around his head.

He was surprised the third man hadn't come to check things out after the sound of the gunshots. If Eli had been leading this team of operatives, he would've been on that.

Something was up. This was out of character and training.

Maybe the third man had bugged out. Nothing would surprise him now that he knew the true nature of his employer—or rather, *former* employer.

He stepped over the dead man and into the living room. The television was off and it was eerily quiet in the room.

There was a man was sitting in a chair in the corner. Saliva was dripping down from his mouth and there was a long, oozing laceration around his throat indicative of strangulation. His face was a bit swollen and languid, but Eli recognized him.

Frogger.

He looked·away from his friend's body.

His going rogue had cost Frogger his life.

Fury raced through him. His former bosses would pay. One way or another, he would never let them get away with coming after them.

"Brother," Eli said, his voice barely above a whisper as he genuflected out of respect for his fallen comrade.

"Brother? Is this what you Watch Dogs do to your *brothers*?" Stepping out of the shadows behind Frogger was Chad. "I hate to imagine what you've done to my sister."

Of course, he would think he was still working for Watch Dogs, and therefore an enemy. Eli dropped his gun and put his hands up. "No, man. I would never hurt Zoey. I love her."

As Zoey stepped into the room, Chad spotted her. "Zoey? I'm so glad you're okay," Chad sighed with relief. "You are okay, aren't you?" He nudged his chin in Eli's direction like a protective father.

"I'm fine," Zoey said, looking over at Eli. "In

fact, if we get out of here alive, *we* will be even more than fine."

Eli couldn't control the wide grin that took over his face. Was that her way of saying she still wanted to marry him? Damn, he hoped so. He wanted to spend every minute of every single day with her... the woman who had saved his life.

Eli gave him a nod. "It's okay, Chad. We were here to rescue you."

Chad chuckled as he stepped around the dead man and stripped off his leather gloves. "And yet, here I am saving you."

"This fight isn't over yet," Eli said, picking up his gun.

"The place should be clear." Chad walked over and took the gun from him. "I was hoping this would prove useful in case of emergencies." He pointed to a small indentation in the gun's handle.

"Is that our gun? The one with the GPS?" Zoey asked, reaching for it. Chad gave it back to her.

"It was how I tracked the crew after me. I left it behind when Shaye and I bugged out. I knew that they had our location and I was hoping to use it to find whoever was tracking me."

"So, you knew that there was money on your head?" Eli asked.

Chad nodded. "Yeah, sucks to know I'm worth a hell of a lot more dead than I am alive. I was half tempted to stage my own death and cash in on the bounty."

Zoey smirked as she glanced in Eli's direction, then to Chad. "Why don't you? We could give the money to Shaye. It seems only right, and it would be kinda perfect if her father *paid* for his sins."

"Actually, that was what the wire transfer was for. I knew you'd be okay with me helping out my friend's family. Raj's parents lost everything, their business, their son and any chance they had of survival, all thanks to the prime minister." Chad sighed. "I will pay the company back. It was just the only place I knew I could pull a large sum of coded money and also let you know that I was alive."

Zoey nodded. "Don't worry about the company's money. Right now, I think we have a death to stage. That is, if you're in."

"I'm in. Raj's family and Shaye...they are going to need help getting on their feet," Chad said, walking over and taking Shaye's hand. "What do you say? Want to make your father give something back for all that he's taken from you?"

Shaye's eyes welled up with tears. "I... You guys... You be careful when dealing with my father."

"We will be. And you will get what you deserve for everything your father has put you through." Chad put his arm over her shoulder and hugged her tight to him. "One thing about us Martins, we believe in picking the right side—the side of justice—especially when that involves taking out the bastards who wish to hurt the people we love."

Chapter Twenty-Two

It didn't take a hell of a lot of work to get a little DNA evidence and "prove" that Chad had been taken out by a contract killer.

The money was in their bank account the very next day when they arrived back at the Widow Maker Ranch. Hopefully their home would be safe now that the hit had been closed on Chad's head, but they were hardly out of the woods. If Zoey had done everything right, Bayural was probably looking for them somewhere in the middle of Norway right now and anyone who had been tracking Chad was off the scent.

Only time would tell.

She sat back on the velvet sofa and looked over the top of her computer at Eli. He was staring at her, making her wonder if it was the feel of his gaze that had made her look up in the first place.

"You gonna stare at me all day?" she asked with a smile.

"If I get my way, I sure as hell will," he said. "What are you doing?"

"Making sure that everything is clear. Just made it look like Shaye was taking a flight out of Sitges headed to Paris. She is going to send her father a letter ceding from the family." She made a long face. "It's going to be harder for her than she anticipates, I think. She's gone through a lot."

"I know. But she is a strong woman, kind of like you." Eli stood up and walked over. She gently pushed her computer closed and moved it off her lap. Then he extended his hand. "Will you do me the honor?"

She slipped her hand into his and he helped her to her feet. "Where are we going? Am I going to need to grab my jacket?"

He laughed, giving her a soft smile. "That's not what I meant."

She stopped. He wasn't going to do what she thought he was going to do, was he? Her entire body clenched with anticipation.

He dropped to one knee. Reaching into his pocket, he pulled out a red velvet box. "I had this made especially for you a long time ago. I've kept it with me ever since. Just like you, it's one of a kind."

He opened up the ring box. Inside was a simple platinum band with a sapphire set into its center.

He must have been carrying it for her for some time. The thought melted her. Even when she was adrift, he had loved her. And she had loved him.

"Will you marry me?"

"I love you, Eli. I love you so much. I'll love you until I take my last breath."

"Is that a yes?" he asked, looking up at her.

"A deal is a deal," she said, giving him a playful smile. "We got out of there alive. I mean…thanks to me, but…yes, I will marry you."

As he moved to stand up, she stopped him and put her hand over her mouth. "Wait."

"What, honey?" he asked, taking her hands from her face and holding them. "What's wrong?"

"What about trying again…you know…for a family?" She wasn't sure what she wanted him to say. And she wasn't sure she was ready to go down that road once again.

He stood up and wrapped his arms around her. "For now, all I want is for you to be my forever. I am yours and you are mine," he whispered into her hair. "If someday it happens, then yes…and if we choose not to, then no. But no matter what life brings, I just want us to face it together."

Together. There was no sweeter word. Or perhaps there was one—*forever.*

* * * * *

Look for Protective Operation, *the next book in the Stealth series by Danica Winters, available March 2020 wherever Harlequin Intrigue books and ebooks are sold.*

COMING NEXT MONTH FROM

⊕ HARLEQUIN

INTRIGUE

Available February 18, 2020

#1911 BEFORE HE VANISHED
A Winchester, Tennessee Thriller • by Debra Webb
Halle Lane's best friend disappeared twenty-five years ago, but when Liam Hart arrives in Winchester, Halle's certain he's the boy she once knew. As the pair investigates Liam's mysterious past, can they uncover the truth before a killer buries all evidence of the boy Halle once loved?

#1912 MYSTERIOUS ABDUCTION
A Badge of Honor Mystery • by Rita Herron
Cora Reeves's baby went missing in a fire five years ago, but she's convinced the child is still out there. When Sheriff Jacob Maverick takes on the cold case, new leads begin to appear—as well as new threats.

#1913 UNDERCOVER REBEL
The Mighty McKenzies Series • by Lena Diaz
Homeland Security agent Ian McKenzie has been working undercover to break up a human-trafficking ring, but when things go sideways, Shannon Murphy is suddenly caught in the crosshairs. Having only recently learned the truth about Ian, can Shannon trust him with her life?

#1914 SOUTH DAKOTA SHOWDOWN
A Badlands Cops Novel • by Nicole Helm
Sheriff Jamison Wyatt has spent his life helping his loved ones escape his father's ruthless gang. Yet when Liza Dean's sister finds herself caught in the gang's most horrifying crime yet, they'll have to infiltrate the crime syndicate and find her before it's too late.

#1915 PROTECTIVE OPERATION
A Stealth Novel • by Danica Winters
Shaye Geist and Chad Martin are both hiding from powerful enemies in the wilds of Montana, and when they find an abandoned baby, they must join forces. Can they keep themselves and the mysterious child safe—even as enemies close in on all sides?

#1916 CRIMINAL ALLIANCE
Texas Brothers of Company B • by Angi Morgan
There's an algorithm that could destroy Dallas, and only FBI operative Therese Ortis and Texas Ranger Wade Hamilton can find and stop it. But going undercover is always dangerous. Can they accomplish their goal before they're discovered? _____

YOU CAN FIND MORE INFORMATION ON UPCOMING HARLEQUIN TITLES, FREE EXCERPTS AND MORE AT HARLEQUIN.COM.

HICNM02

*Sheriff Jamison Wyatt has never forgotten Liza Dean,
the one who got away. But now she's back, and she needs
his help to find her sister. They'll have to infiltrate a crime
syndicate, but once they're on the inside, will they
be able to get back out?*

Read on for a sneak preview of
South Dakota Showdown *by Nicole Helm.*

Chapter One

Bonesteel, South Dakota, wasn't even a dot on most maps, which
was precisely why Jamison Wyatt enjoyed being its attached
officer. Though he was officially a deputy with the Valiant County
Sheriff's Department, as attached officer his patrol focused on
Bonesteel and its small number of residents.

One of six brothers, he wasn't the only Wyatt who acted as an
officer of the law—but he was the only man who'd signed up for
the job of protecting Bonesteel.

He'd grown up in the dangerous, unforgiving world of a biker
gang run by his father. The Sons of the Badlands were a cutthroat
group who'd been wreaking havoc on the small communities of
South Dakota—just like this one—for decades.

Luckily, Jamison had spent the first five years of his life on his
grandmother's ranch before his mother had fully given in to Ace
Wyatt and moved them into the fold of the nomadic biker gang.

Through tenacity and grit Jamison had held on to a belief in
right and wrong that his grandmother had instilled in him in those
early years. When his mother had given birth to son after son on the
inside of the Sons, Jamison had known he would get them out—
and he had, one by one—and escape to their grandmother's ranch
situated at the very edge of Valiant County.

It was Jamison's rough childhood in the gang and the immense responsibility he'd placed on himself to get his brothers away from it that had shaped him into a man who took everything perhaps a shade too seriously. Or so his brothers said.

Jamison had no regrets on that score. Seriousness kept people safe. He was old enough now to enjoy the relative quiet of patrolling a small town like Bonesteel. He had no desire to see lawbreaking. He'd seen enough. But he had a deep, abiding desire to make sure everything was right.

So it was odd to be faced with a clear B and E just a quarter past nine at night on the nearly deserted streets. Maybe if it had been the general store or gas station, he might have understood. But the figure was trying to break into his small office attached to city hall.

It was bold and ridiculous enough to be moderately amusing. Probably a drunk, he thought. Maybe the…woman—yes, it appeared to be a woman—was drunk and looking to sleep it off.

When he did get calls, they were often alcohol related and mostly harmless, as this appeared to be.

Since Jamison was finishing up his normal last patrol for the night, he was on foot. He walked slowly over, keeping his steps light and his body in the shadows. The streets were quiet, having long since been rolled up for the night.

Still, the woman worked on his doorknob. If she was drunk, she was awfully steady for one. Either way, she didn't look to pose much of a threat.

He stepped out of the shadow. "Typically people who break and enter are better at picking a lock."

The woman stopped what she was doing—but she hadn't jumped or shrieked or even stumbled. She just stilled.

Don't miss
South Dakota Showdown *by Nicole Helm,*
available March 2020 wherever
Harlequin Intrigue books and ebooks are sold.

Harlequin.com

Love Harlequin romance?

DISCOVER.

Be the first to find out about promotions,
news and exclusive content!

f Facebook.com/HarlequinBooks

🐦 Twitter.com/HarlequinBooks

📷 Instagram.com/HarlequinBooks

📌 Pinterest.com/HarlequinBooks

ReaderService.com

EXPLORE.

Sign up for the Harlequin e-newsletter and
download a free book from any series at
TryHarlequin.com

CONNECT.

Join our Harlequin community to
share your thoughts and connect
with other romance readers!
Facebook.com/groups/HarlequinConnection

Heartfelt or suspenseful, inspiring or passionate, Harlequin has your happily-ever-after.

With new books published every month, you are sure to find the satisfying escape you know you deserve.

HNEWS2020